BY THE SAME AUTHOR

Pip and Emma

(A Margaret K. McElderry Book)

Shadow and Light

Shadow and Light

Katharine Jay Bacon

MARGARET K. MCELDERRY BOOKS
NEW YORK

Margaret K. McElderry Books
Macmillan Publishing Company
866 Third Avenue
New York, NY 10022
Collier Macmillan Canada, Inc.

Composition by Maryland Linotype Composition Company
Baltimore, Maryland
Printed and bound by R. R. Donnelley & Sons
Harrisonburg, Virginia
Designed by Barbara A. Fitzsimmons

First Edition
Printed in the United States of America

10 9 8 7 6 5 4 3 2 1

Library of Congress Cataloging-in-Publication Data

Bacon, Katharine.
Shadow and light.

Summary: Fifteen-year-old Emma looks forward to
spending the summer on her beloved grandmother's
Vermont farm but is devastated to learn that her
grandmother is fatally ill and wants Emma to help
her live her last months in peace and dignity.
[1. Grandmothers—Fiction. 2. Death—Fiction.
3. Farm life—Fiction] I. Title.
PZ7.B1343Sh   1987   [Fic]   86-23789
ISBN 0-689-50431-4

*For my sisters and brother
and
for my daughters and son*

Contents

PART ONE

How odd. Emma, staring impatiently out the window of the bus, saw her grandmother's familiar figure standing at the Winslow station, but something about her was different. Then their eyes met, Gee's face lit up, and the momentary impression of otherness vanished.

Perched on the edge of her seat, Emma counted once again the various bags and parcels and bits of clothing she had been clutching for the past twenty minutes. The bus came to a full stop, the doors whooshed open, and she jumped down the two metal steps, dropped her bundles, and flung herself into Gee's arms.

"I thought we'd never, ever, *ever* get here," she said, beaming at her grandmother, the town of Winslow, the glorious afternoon, at life in general. The outside corners of Emma's long brown eyes turned down when she smiled, casting lines that accentuated her high cheekbones.

"Oh, darling, darling, it is so good to see you," said Gee, releasing the tall, slim figure. She smiled, then turned and pointed. "Look! There's your trunk."

Throwing her gear into the car, Emma could

hardly refrain from snapping at Gee to hurry *up*, so great was her impatience to get to Bell Brook Farm; but once they pulled away from the station she settled down and let loose the flood of questions that had been building inside her.

"How *fat* is Chloe?" she asked.

"Huge."

"And the foal is due on or about the Fourth of July, right?" (Knowing perfectly well that it was.)

"Right, pumpkin."

"Oh, Gee, what if it comes right spang *on* the Fourth? We could call it Yankee Doodle if it's a colt, and what do you think of Macaroni if it's a filly?"

"Not a great deal," said Gee with a smile.

Emma laughed. "I knew you'd say that. Maybe Liberty would be better for a girl. Oh, *dear*—if it comes on the Fourth, what'll we do about Mrs. Archer's picnic?"

In all her fifteen years Emma had only missed this annual event once.

"Why don't we wait and see," Gee suggested, stopping at Winslow's one traffic light. "Foals don't take long to come as a rule, and Chloe's good at it. With a little luck you'll have your cake and eat it, too."

Emma tapped her foot, waiting for the light to turn.

"Do you think Mrs. Tig"—Mrs. Tiggywinkle was her elderly black pony—"do you think Mrs.

Tig will still remember me? Is she too old to use this year? Should we start some of the little ones on her, the ones that are too little for the new pony, I mean?"

"Yes. No. Maybe," answered Gee, imitating Emma's rapid-fire voice and putting the car in gear.

"Oh, and Gee, what about Hal, will you let me ride him tomorrow? Is he fit? How about I get him in shape for you—"

"Now, whoa. I've been thinking about that. As a matter of fact, along with your playing midwife to Chloe and running the whole barn menagerie, I've decided to put you in charge of Hal, too, in case I don't get around to riding him enough this summer. The garden's already ahead of me."

For once Emma was struck dumb. After a moment she said, "*You* are letting *me* take over *Hal?* Good grief. All this and heaven, too."

Thoughtfully she drew up her knees and hugged them.

"You wait, Gee. You won't regret it. I'll take such good care of those horses and ponies and sheep and lambs and kittens and—oh dear—even the geese."

Emma was scared of the geese, but even the thought of having to deal with the fierce old gander could not dampen her ardor.

"I'm going to do the *best* job. And you can lie in bed late and I'll bring you breakfast on a tray—"

5

"Not quite, my dear," said Gee, a trifle sharply, Emma thought. "I am simply turning over the barn work for your project. Of course it will help me, too—and working with Hal should get you extra credit."

Part of the reason Emma's parents were letting her spend the whole summer at Bell Brook Farm was a statewide competition for high school juniors on the best summer work project and report.

"Now remember: organize the work, Em, plan your time, *pay attention*, make notes, even, as you do in school. Be methodical, like me."

They both giggled. Gee fought a losing battle with paperwork; in an effort to get control of it she had divided her file cabinet into four sections: A for Animals, G for Grandchildren, I for Important, and S for Scary.

"How many lambs this year?" Emma began again.

"Eleven, starting in mid-February. The newest one came last night; tiny, black, and late—a ewe lamb."

"And what about human babies? Who's having one this year?"

"Pam. Number three for them."

"And for you? No, don't tell me, I can count." Emma whistled. "More grandchildren than lambs, that's for sure."

"I know. I can hardly believe it myself," said Gee. "And to think Dan isn't even married yet.

Heaven knows where it will end." She gave a rueful grunt of laughter. "When Pip and you were born I thought I was far too young to be a grandmother, but . . . time flies, it surely flies . . . how I wish your grandfather were here to see you all. . . ."

"Oh, Gee," said Emma, quickly changing the subject. She saw a shadow cross her grandmother's face at the mention of her husband, who had died so many years ago, and it upset her to think of Gee being sad. "Oh, Gee, I can't wait to show you the present I brought you. It's a surprise, though. I won't tell you what it is, so don't ask."

They entered the village of Doe's Crossing and Emma fell silent, her angular face drawn tight as she focused all her attention on familiar landmarks. But when they turned into the dirt road and started up the last five miles to Bell Brook Farm, she smiled at the remembered jiggle of the car and the cloud of dust it raised around them. The low late-afternoon sun dappled the washboard road as it followed Bell Brook through woods and little meadows, past farms, over rumbling wooden bridges, in and out of light and shadow all the way.

Rounding the last curve at the foot of Gee's hill, Emma unfolded her legs and leaned forward. "What a day, Gee," she breathed happily. Far up the hillside she glimpsed, through a break in the trees, the farm basking in its sunny meadow. "What a day to come home."

They both knew what she meant. Real home was

in West Virginia, but Emma and her older brother Pip had been spending all or part of their summers at Bell Brook Farm ever since they could remember, and so it was their second home.

Up the ever-narrowing road Gee drove, taking the bumps skillfully, shifting down as the grade steepened. At the hairpin turn into her lane she drew up alongside the mailbox and pulled it open.

"Junk. Junk. Junk," she muttered irritably, sweeping an armload of assorted envelopes and flyers and catalogs onto her lap.

"But, Gee,"—Emma flipped through the jumble —"look, here's a letter from Pam, and some bills— you'd better not throw them out—and this one looks real,"—she held up a long white envelope— "I mean, it may not be handwritten but at least it's typed on a real machine. Let's see, it's from a James Fothergill, Attorney, Winslow, Vermont. It says 'Personal'."

Gee took the letter from her and laid it on top of the pile she had tossed to the floor. Before the car started forward again, Emma opened her door.

"I'll walk up," she said, beginning to get out. Then, aware again of a different look to her grandmother—Was she tired? After all she did get up very early—Emma climbed back onto the seat and hugged her.

"Leave the bags, Gee Golly Gosh. I'll unload everything."

She waited until the car disappeared around a curve before starting up the little road. It was a narrow lane, sunk low between ferny banks, and a strip of grass grew in the middle. Birches and maples on either side followed the old stone walls that early farmers had built with the rocks they dug while clearing land for pasture. But Gee's mother, Mamie, had sold her cows many years ago, and now the pasture to the left was overgrown with white pine and juniper, blackberry bushes and hardhack. The great hay meadow across the lane to the south, however, stretched all the way up to the house and disappeared over the verge of the hill.

Emma took her time, steeping herself in the scene around her. The afternoon sun cast long shadows across the meadow from the woods at its western edge, but as the land sloped upward light fell over the hay and turned it, thought Emma, into a billowing buff-colored sea.

She rounded the curve and there was Mount Ascutney, blue and stately above the undulating lines of distant treetops. Emma loved Ascutney. It reigned as a solitary beacon over Bell Brook valley and the surrounding countryside, and after rain or snow neighbors, discussing the weather, asked each other, "Is the mountain out yet?"

At the foot of the final rise to the house, she paused and looked up, searching the branches of the largest of the maples until she found the old tree house. Built by Pip four years ago when he was thirteen and she was eleven, it was spacious, ramshackle, surprisingly sturdy. Pip had thrown himself into its creation, ordering her and their friend Joey about like slaves.

That was when they were all still children; lately their younger cousins had begun to take it over. It gave Emma quite a pang to outgrow the tree house, until she reminded herself how exciting her next birthday would be.

On the Labor Day weekend, just before returning to West Virginia, she was going to celebrate her sixteenth birthday. It had been in the works for a year. As she was the eldest of Gee's granddaughters, this would be a special family event, almost a rite of passage, and all the aunts and all their husbands and children, and her uncle Dan, Gee's only son and youngest child, and his girlfriend, and many of Gee's neighbors, who had known Emma forever, had all promised to come to the party.

Emma marveled to think she would be sixteen. Always it had seemed a charmed age to her, a watershed of sorts; ever since early childhood she had said to herself, "When I am sixteen. . . ." Now that the magic year was nearly upon her, she was not entirely sure whether or not she was glad. Well, September was a long way off.

She squinted up at the tree house, remembering

the times she had spent there, playing, smoking, camping out, daydreaming, sulking, reading, and hiding. From the tree house she had observed many of the goings-on at Bell Brook Farm: visitors arriving and departing; babies and toddlers rolling and staggering across the lawn; heated games of croquet; Gee, dancing in the garden once, when she thought she was alone; cross words as well as laughter; arguments and courtships; once Emma observed a beautiful married second cousin weeping in the barnyard as she talked to Gee, who stood chewing her lip and looking sad.

But her most vivid memories were of all the aunts and, as time went on, their husbands, erupting in spontaneous and gleeful outbursts of energy: rough-and-tumble games of Frisbee, football, kite flying in the meadow after the hay was cut. The four aunts were her mother's younger sisters—Lexy, Pam, Sukie, and Libba. Occasionally their "baby" brother—six-foot Dan—came home with his handsome Navy friends and joined them at play; those were enchanted times, but the aunts, so near and yet so far in age from Emma, were in a category all to themselves.

Perhaps she would decide to sleep in the tree house on the night before her birthday; that might be a fitting way to bring childhood to an end.

Emma started up the rise, then left the lane just before it reached the crest of the hill and quickly cut up the bank to the lawn in front of the house. There it sat—inviting, intimate, safe, a small brick house with a long, white clapboard wing. Behind it and to either side towered centuries-old maples; to the west and curving around behind, the apple orchard; beyond it, the pond. To the east, at the foot of the lawn and below Mamie's old garden, the lane continued to the barn and Emma's domain. She gazed down at it, sorely tempted; but remembering that Gee looked tired and might need help, she turned back to the house, glowing pink now in the light of the descending sun.

Summer-evening stillness lay over the farm, the shadows lengthened. With a little surge of ecstasy Emma bounded across the lawn and up the wide stone steps and in the front door.

As she burst into the house, the dogs ran yelping from the kitchen. Recognizing Emma, they looked embarrassed and slithered across the hall floor, scattering the rugs left and right, to fling themselves upon her—old Witch, the terrier, half-blind, half-deaf, and fully as mean as ever; and Dumbo, the big, woolly, brown poodle with the uncut tail. Emma grinned and knelt to greet them and then passed on into the kitchen, looking for Gee.

She was in the Music Room, beyond the kitchen. Now an informal family room, it was still called the Music Room because nearly sixty years ago

Gee's mother had bought one of the early wind-up gramophones and kept it out there. Gee grew up playing crackling recordings of the hit songs of her youth. In time an upright piano and an ancient cousin's even older cello lent the name of the room more authenticity. Now there was a very good stereo system and Gee played very good music on it, but she still had a fondness for the oldtimers. Her favorite was a Fred Astaire show called *Follow the Fleet*—especially the song "We Saw the Sea."

Emma came to the doorway and saw Gee standing in front of her famous file cabinet with a letter in one hand and a frown on her face.

"What is it this time, Gee? I or S?" Emma asked.

Gee looked up and smiled quickly. She laid the letter down on top of the cabinet. "A little of each," she answered, gathering up the rest of the day's mail. "Hungry, pumpkin? It's getting on for suppertime."

"Oh, wait, Gee, stay there! I want to give you your present."

Emma ran out the Music Room door to the car parked outside and rooted around in one of her bags. In a moment she returned, carrying a small package, which she held out to her grandmother.

"You look like the cat that swallowed the canary," said Gee, taking it from her.

"I am," said Emma. "Hurry up and open it."

Gee shook the package, trying to guess what it held, then she undid the ribbon and wrapping paper and, still mystified, opened the little cardboard box. Immediately her eyes filled with tears.

"Oh, Em," she cried, hugging her hard. "Oh, Em—" She laughed and brushed at her eyes. "You really took me by surprise, darling. I'm *thrilled*. Quick, let's put it on!"

Last summer Gee had played "We Saw the Sea" a great deal, constantly bemoaning its crackly condition. Emma vowed to herself that she would find a way to transcribe the song, clean, onto a cassette. It turned out to be quite a complicated undertaking, because the song was so old. When the music store back home finally found a barely used record and put it onto a tape, Emma was extremely pleased, both with herself and the result.

Gee started the machine and out into the room floated the voices of the young sailors. The notes were clear and true, and Gee's eyes sparkled with delight. Spontaneously she and Emma began to dance around the Music Room, singing the chorus aloud:

Sailing, sailing home *again,*

they roared together,

To see the girls upon the village green.
Then across the foam again,
To see the other seas we haven't seen.

They were both quite breathless at the end.

Gee sank back onto the sofa and said, "Oh, Em, that *is* a treat. However did you track it down?"

"It took all winter," said Emma smugly. "*Nobody'd* ever heard of it. Why is that record so special for you, anyway, Gee? Because your father was a sea captain and you spent a lot of time on boats?"

Gee ran her hand through her hair. (How gray she's got, Emma thought.) "Perhaps. I don't know. I like the tune and I like Fred Astaire and I like the idea of sailing *home* again, and most of all it reminds me of when I was a girl like you."

She reached over and put her finger on the end of Emma's nose. "Now go to the barn, pumpkin. I can practically see you jumping out of your skin to be there. I'll start supper."

When Emma entered the barnyard, Chloe, bulging with foal, raised her head and whickered, and Hal jogged over to the gate, sleek, handsome, royal. Emma patted him and fed his vanity with praise, while the two ponies and Gee's aged thoroughbred, Ben, watched her from the shed. In a moment one of the ponies ambled over to the gate, bared her teeth at Hal, and laid her nose on Emma's shoulder. Emma felt a lump in her throat.

"Hello, Mrs. Tig," she said, hugging her.

When she had had her fill of the horses and re-established her presence among them, she went into the lower level of the barn, just to check out the rest of the livestock. A neighbor had done afternoon chores while Gee met Emma's bus. Coming out of the long late light, she had to stop for a moment until her eyes adjusted to the gloom.

It was cool down here as always. Two young half-wild cats skittered in front of her and vanished up into the beams over the stalls. Out the door at the far end Emma could see the little flock of sheep and older lambs lying under a maple. Just as she remembered that there was a new lamb on the place she heard a saucy bleat and the low answering grunt of its dam, and she went eagerly to the lambing pen. Once again she found it quite impossible to believe that anything could be as picture-perfect as a newborn lamb.

Emma was about to go in and pick it up when a fierce rustle made her look around to see the geese bearing down on her; in the nick of time she leaped for the ladder to the next floor and climbed out of their reach.

Upstairs, on the main floor, the barn was still daylit. Emma went into the huge loft, nearly emptied of last year's hay and deep in shadow, and climbed onto a pile of the remaining bales. In the peak of the roof the hay door hung open, and through it she watched the sky change before her eyes, giving way from day to dusk, as the sun—now sunk below the northwest hill behind the house—

cast its last glow before evening fell. First, pink tinged the square above her, then a hint of green, and finally, without her being aware of how or when it happened, an almost colorless blue. True dark would not come for an hour or more.

Sitting cross-legged on the hay, Emma thought at first she was wholly content, and then she squinted in an effort to identify the faint unease that niggled at her. Something was out of place in her heaven. She pondered what it could be.

She was conscious of having returned to a world in which she was totally at home. It was a world she had looked forward to throughout the school year, a world in which she felt safe, competent, engaged. She didn't feel different, she just felt like herself. And yet at school she knew she was different from the other girls in her class; she knew she was the only one who cared more about horses than boys. They lived in a different world from Emma.

This summer at Bell Brook Farm, while she was immersed in her project, should she maybe try to change her attitude, venturing away from the safe world of the barn? Should she try to be more open to other aspects of growing up, now that she was nearly sixteen? Was this what niggled at her? Maybe. And yet, the ever-so-slight anxiety still stirred. What could it be?

Just then Chloe neighed down in the barnyard,

the sound trumpeting through the early twilight, and Emma heard Hal galloping from a far corner of the pasture. She put her thoughts aside and rushed out of the barn and around the corner to watch Hal, marveling at his beauty. When Gee rang the cowbell for supper, Emma climbed the barn gate, ravenous, her delight fully restored, and ran up the hill to the house.

In the middle of supper the telephone rang, and Gee got up to answer it in the hall, pulling the kitchen door shut behind her. Emma was surprised to notice that Gee hadn't touched her food; as a rule her grandmother was the first one to finish. In fact, remembered Emma with a grin, once Gee had served eleven plates around the table, then taken her place, picked up her knife and fork, and said, "On your mark, get set, *go*!"

"—go," said Gee on the telephone, and Emma realized the door had swung open. "I can't bear to have it go, Jim. We'll have to think of some way—"

Something in her grandmother's voice made Emma stop chewing and pay attention.

"Yes, and I do agree it's just as well to have things settled."

Emma swallowed the food she had been holding in her mouth in order to hear better.

"You wrote in your letter," Gee was saying, "that the cost of probate might necessitate the sale. . . ."

What kind of language is that? Emma wondered.

"Okay, Jim, tomorrow, then. Bring all that awful paperwork with you—" She laughed, a little hollowly, Emma thought. "Yes, I picked her up this afternoon." The voice lightened. "I feel like a new person, just having her around. . . . Good night, Jim, see you at three tomorrow."

"Jim who?" Emma asked when Gee came back into the kitchen.

"My new lawyer, Jim Fothergill. He's bringing some papers tomorrow for me to go over and sign. You'll like him, I think. He's a consultant for a big New York firm but lives up here." She sat down and took up her fork and speared some salad. "Go on about the barn, Em. Isn't that new lamb adorable?"

"I'll say. I was just going in to pick her up when the geese came after me and I had to run for my life up the ladder. . . . I'd forgotten how big the hayloft looks when it's nearly empty. Mysterious. I sat there for a while and watched the sky."

Emma took her plate to the sink, then went to the refrigerator to refill her glass of milk. Should she talk to Gee? she wondered. Emma was a very private person; but she trusted her grandmother, so when she returned to the table she said, "You know, Gee, a lot of girls in my class have boyfriends—most of them, in fact. In fact, they've had boyfriends for years. Some of them are pretty far into it—" she felt her cheeks coloring—"having boyfriends."

Dumbo came and sat next to her and laid his head on her lap. Avoiding looking at her grandmother, Emma played with his curly brown ears and said, "Minnie Rockenheimer dropped out of school this year to have a baby. A *baby*, Gee. She's only fifteen, my age, in fact I'll be sixteen before her."

She looked up and found Gee's eyes upon her, soft with affection. She had laid down her fork, the salad uneaten.

"I've got lots of friends who are boys," Emma went on. "Lots. And I like Pip's friends, too . . . except for one."

She paused, remembering him unwillingly, with a familiar little shudder of distaste, and the intimacies she had allowed him once, when she was only twelve and he fourteen.

"But I think," she hurried on "I know—some of the girls, even my good friends—even my best friend, Mary Jo—think I'm kind of backward not to have a real boyfriend. They tease me about the riding and the horses. . . ."

"Well, there's teasing and teasing," said Gee, when Emma remained silent. "They also elected you vice-president of your class, so they can't be too down on you for preferring horses to boys. I'm just surprised you're the only one who does. It's quite a common phenomenon." She smiled at Emma and laid her hand over hers. "Truly, I wouldn't worry about it, darling. People grow at different rates. Time, and a light heart. . . . Enjoy each day, each moment, one at a time."

"Yes, well, to tell you the truth, that's what I already decided, down in the barn . . . oh, Gee, I am glad to be here. I've been looking forward to this summer so much."

She looked at her grandmother, expecting to find her pleasure mirrored, and was puzzled by a look on her face, a look that somehow reminded Emma of the figure at the bus station. Gee smiled— rather too quickly, as she had in the Music Room— and said, exaggerating, as was her wont, "My word, it's pitch-dark in here. Go switch on the light, honey, and let's get these dishes done. It's time you unloaded the car, too."

After she had lugged all her gear upstairs, dragging the trunk bumpety-bump over each step because she refused to allow Gee to help, Emma sat down on her little bed under the eave and let the dim twilight, which filled the familiar room, wrap itself around her. Through the north window loomed the dark silhouette of the hill behind the house; through the open eastern one came muted sounds from the barn.

She had considered asking Gee if she could have Pip's room next door—it faced south and east and was thus sunnier, and it had the view of Ascutney —because he was going to be here so little this summer since he was being a counselor at camp. Now she was glad she hadn't. This was *her* room when she was at Bell Brook Farm. Hers and hers alone. From time to time Pip had to share his, when the house was full, because there were two beds in there. It would have been a great mistake to switch.

Emma liked the hurly-burly at Bell Brook Farm when family and friends were there; she liked people in general, especially the mixed ages that came and went in Gee's house, and she was very fond of all the aunts and Dan and amused by her younger cousins. Equally, as she grew older, she liked the times of peace and quiet, when she could have the farm, and Gee, to herself.

In a very different way from the barn, her little room was a refuge, where sometimes she read far into the night after the rest of the household went to bed, or wrote page after page in her journal, knowing it was safe from prying eyes.

Some years ago Pip had called it her Inner Sanctum, and Emma thought that sounded marvelous, so she got her brother to spell it for her and made a sign and hung it on the door. Only after he left the house did she look up the meaning in the dictionary.

Now, through the hot-air register under her bed, Emma could hear her grandmother moving around the kitchen beneath Pip's room and hers. That was how she always knew Gee was up in the morning: There would be the scrabble of the dogs' claws across the linoleum floor, then Gee's slippers scuffing along behind them, followed almost immediately by a sharp hiccoughing sound, which meant that she had opened the door of the ancient refrigerator. No one had ever figured out what made it do that. The refrigerator belted out its merry little cry at odd moments during the day, subsiding into silence in the evening.

Well, Emma thought, suddenly tired from her long trip and the pent-up excitement of beginning this special summer at Bell Brook Farm, I'd better unpack. She got up and turned on the light.

Emma was fastidious in many ways. She still liked the bottom sheet on her bed to be drawn absolutely tight; unlike Pip, she kept her drawers tidy and her clothes hung on hangers in the closet, instead of lying in heaps on the floor.

When she came to the pile of T-shirts in her trunk, she pulled open the bottom drawer of her bureau and froze. There, sitting up in the back of the drawer, regarding her reproachfully, was a small gray mouse.

Emma backed away. She knelt down, stuck her head under the bed, and called in a hoarse whisper, "Gee!"

The top of Gee's head appeared directly below; she looked up.

"What, pumpkin?"

"Gee—there's a *mouse* in my drawer. He's just sitting there, like he owned the place—"

"As though," Gee corrected.

"Oh, Gee, never mind grammar now. Come *do* something."

Gee laughed and moved out of view. "I'm coming up anyway, but you might try stamping at it."

Emma returned to the drawer. The mouse was still there; he was cleaning his paws and did not even look up at her. She stamped her foot tentatively. The mouse, to Emma's stunned disbelief, stamped back, then returned to his ablutions.

Just then Gee appeared in the room, marched firmly to the bureau, and banged her hand on the top of it; and the mouse scampered out of sight through a crack in the back of the drawer.

Emma sighed with relief, then asked nervously, "*Now* where is he?"

"Gone to join the gang in the attic, I suppose," Gee said, sitting down on Emma's bed. "They're all over the house this year. You should have heard them last winter—they sounded like a herd of elephants running over the ceiling.

"In fact, one evening I watched a rerun of "Wild World of Animals", about the elephants in Kenya, about how the government and the farmers and the environmentalists and everyone got together to try *not* to have to kill them—setting aside huge tracts of land for them and all that—but still the elephants left their own territory and trampled the farmers' crops over and over, until killing them was the only thing left if the farmers were to survive." She sighed. "Complicated."

"Still, what are you going to do about all these mice?"

"I just wish they could *read*."

"Why read?"

"I could leave messages for them saying, 'Go away or I'll have to set out poison.' Everyone says 'Get a house cat,' but with Dumbo around that's out of the question, and I just can't bring myself to set out poison." She got up and gave Emma a hug on her way to the door. "Good night, pumpkin."

"I don't know, Gee," said Emma, picking up the pile of T-shirts, "I bet that mouse could read."

Once all her things were put away and her room was in order, Emma undressed, turned out the light, and, crawling carefully between the sheets, arranged herself comfortably in bed. She lay and reviewed the day, trying to ignore the little flutter of anxiety in her belly but recognizing nonetheless that despite her happiness to be back at Bell Brook Farm, despite her enthusiasm for the summer project, something was still bothering her, and she didn't think it had a thing to do with horses or boys.

Whatever it was had started the minute the bus drew into Winslow and had been coming and going in fits and starts ever since. Now she faced it. It was Gee. Something was wrong with Gee, though still Emma could not put her finger on it. She began to collect all the little warning signs she had noticed since her arrival. One by one they meant nothing, but added up, they were the cause of her uneasiness.

First of all there was no longer any point denying that Gee looked different: tired, paler, grayer than usual. She didn't eat with her usual relish. In fact, Gee had hardly touched her supper. Against her will Emma forced herself to recall the exact words she had overheard of the telephone conversation with this lawyer—Jim something. Have what things settled? What did probate mean?

Gee had mentioned a letter from him; suddenly Emma knew that must be the letter she was reading in the Music Room, which Emma remembered seeing her leave on top of the file cabinet.

She felt a powerful urge to slip downstairs and read it, but she could not quite bring herself to do that. Because she was too honorable? Or because she was too scared to find out what the letter said? Truly, Emma did not know.

Drowsiness began to wash over her, seeping through her legs, torso, shoulders, until the edges of her body seemed to melt away. When she realized that her door was still open, she was too lazy to get up and close it.

Lying in bed in the dimly lit room, Emma stared absently at the eave over her bed. Just as she was deciding that her eyelids were too heavy to stay open, she saw the spot where years ago a piece of the faded old wallpaper had come loose. The tear was across a shepherdess in a long skirt standing with her flock, and, as a soft current of air blew through the window, the paper lifted and fell, lifted and fell, making it look as though the shepherdess were dancing.

Reassured, Emma fell asleep.

The next morning, while Gee looked on, Emma fed all the animals, tidied the barn, and checked all the tack, finding her way back into a routine that she had followed with her grandmother for years and knew by heart.

On the way back up to the house for breakfast they discussed Emma's schedule for the day, which, she had decided on waking up and announced now to Gee, was going to include preparing the stall Chloe would use to have her foal in—even though it was not due for three weeks—and working Hal on a lunge line. Emma was shocked to learn he had not been ridden all spring.

"Well, you see, pumpkin," said Gee, stopping to lean over the garden wall and pick five peonies, "he sprained his stifle, horsing around in the snow in March, and by the time that healed I was trying to get the garden in. . . ." She laid the peonies in the crook of one arm and they continued on their way. "And, well, what with one thing and another, time slipped by, and I just got lazy, I guess, and decided to leave it all up to you! Maybe by the Fourth of July I'll be caught up and we can ride together." She glanced sideways at Emma and met the long brown eyes regarding her quizzically.

But Emma, seeing Gee early on a fresh June morning, and notwithstanding the improbability of her giving up riding, was reassured by her grandmother's general mien, so she let the matter of Hal's condition drop.

"By the way, I never asked you what Pam's letter said. Is she coming up soon?" Pam was Gee's third daughter and perhaps Emma's favorite aunt.

"Yes, for the Fourth of July, with Libba, and then she and the boys will come back at the end of the summer, to help with the party. I'm still not sure exactly who else will be here for the Fourth. Pip said he might get the weekend off, and there's a chance Cousin Horace will come. Maybe we'll hear today. Be an angel and get the mail for me this afternoon, will you, honey? It's usually there by two-thirty or so. I hate to leave the garden then."

She's sure spending a lot of time in the garden

this year, Emma thought to herself and felt a return of the flutter in her belly, remembering that letter from the lawyer in yesterday's mail.

They went into the house and Gee put on the new tape and hummed along with the song while she arranged the peonies in water and fixed breakfast.

As always when she was at Bell Brook Farm, Emma was hungry. She wolfed down two helpings of pancakes, while Gee drank only some coffee; but, after all, Emma reminded herself, Gee had never gone in much for breakfast. Once again she took comfort in her grandmother's cheerful expression and sprightly step around the kitchen, quite like her old self.

"In all my nearly sixty years I don't believe I have ever seen the peonies so beautiful," said Gee, admiring the bouquet on the windowsill as she dried her cup. "Well, I must call John to discuss the haying. They ought to be starting any day."

When she left the kitchen, Emma went into the Music Room, put the cassette back in its case, and flipped the machine to an FM station. Straightening up, her eye fell upon the open letter on top of the file cabinet at the far end of the room. On a sudden impulse, she went back to the kitchen door and listened for Gee's voice at the hall telephone.

"Well, it's always nice to talk to you, Sonia . . . OK, put him on, please."

Sonia was John's wife. So, she hasn't even started talking to John, thought Emma, and with her heart racing and feeling quite breathless, she ducked back into the Music Room, went quickly to the file cabinet, and picked up the letter. "Dear Gee," she read:

Before getting down to business, I want to tell you how very sorry I was to hear your news. While not taking an unduly pessimistic view, I recognize the gravity of your situation and know that the next two or three months will be tremendously demanding upon your reserves, both physical and mental. Please believe me when I say I want to help you in any way that is within my power to do so.

Now, as to the legal matters—your Eumenides, as you call them. I have reviewed your will and think it is a sound one. There are one or two points we should perhaps discuss when I come out. They concern Bell Brook Farm, and here we come, as you know, to the heart of our legal difficulties.

As your lawyer I must advise you to consider adding a codicil to your will that would direct the sale of the farm at your death (whenever that should occur). I should not urge this course if you would reconsider discussing your health with your children as soon as possible, thereby giving them time—and it takes time—to work out the devise of the farm and enhance the chances of keeping it in the family, which I know is your preference. Otherwise the costs and delays of probate court will—should worse come to worst—invade your rather modest cash assets to a degree that will seriously reduce—

Here Emma heard Gee's footstep in the kitchen. Hastily she replaced the letter and went to the machine to fiddle with the FM knob. She felt cold all over. Hoping her grandmother would not want to tell her when John was coming to mow, she turned the volume up, but Gee simply called "I'll be in the garden, honey." The screen door slammed behind her and Emma found herself alone with her terrifying new knowledge.

She could not bring herself to go back to the letter and finish reading it, for it had assumed a threatening identity of its own: It was her enemy. She stood with her back to the file cabinet and thought, I will go to the barn and when I come up for lunch maybe the letter will have disappeared and I can tell myself I imagined the whole thing.

All morning Emma worked with the horses. Mindfully, she groomed each one, breathing in through her nose and out through her lips, as the summery dust rose in clouds from their hides. Then she treated each hoof with engine oil and combed every mane and tail until even in the dark barn they gleamed, all the time keeping up a steady stream of talk, which varied in tone and content from horse to horse and kept her mind occupied. One by one they passed muster and were led from the crossties in the aisle back to stalls to keep Emma company until she was finished in the barn. Already she could feel the tightness in her chest begin to loosen.

In one corner of the barn was a roomy, fenced-off area with access to its own little yard: the foaling stall. Here Chloe had delivered twice over the years, and now Emma turned her attention upon it to make it ready for the third foal. This would be her first time to be present for the birth, and every time Emma thought about it she felt touched by awe.

Back and forth she pushed the big barrow, filling it with wood shavings and dumping them in the foaling stall. Occasionally the monotony of her task allowed her mind to wander, but she brought it back into focus by counting her steps each way. At last, when the bed was a foot deep, Emma was almost satisfied but decided Chloe should have music when her time came, so she fetched the barn radio from the tack room and hung it on a nail near the stall door, plugging it in to the overhead light.

Next she turned to the tack. Frowning in concentration and whistling tunelessly through her teeth, she took each bridle apart and worked over the leather until it felt like silk in her hand.

"I recognize the gravity of your situation. . . ." The words floated before Emma's inner eye. Immediately she banished them and polished harder. When there was not one scrap left to do and it was only eleven o'clock, she felt a little ripple of anxiety, and she cast about in her mind for another task.

Ah, yes, my schedule, she thought.

Taking down the old blackboard that Gee kept in the tack room to write notes on, she cleaned its gray surface and, lips pursed, methodically wrote down her list of chores. Each day she would record her activity on the slate and transcribe it into her journal.

Now what? she asked herself nervously.

Suddenly her spirits lifted. Of course—Hal.

She led all the other horses out to the orchard pasture before putting on Hal's bridle. Ever since Gee bought him, when he was a yearling, Hal had been a handful; it was only in the last couple of years that Emma had been allowed to ride him at all, as her skill and his manners progressed. Eight years old now, well over sixteen hands tall, bright chestnut with a perfect blaze down his aristocratic nose, Hal exemplified equine elegance.

"The trouble is," Emma whispered through her teeth, as Hal bucked and carried on at the other end of the lunge line, "the trouble is, you know it."

But soon she felt herself attuning to his psyche, as dancing partners must, or trapeze artists, and gratefully she gave herself wholly to the work. With authority, she cracked the lunge whip.

"Enough, Hal! Now *walk!*" And somewhat to her surprise, walk he did, arching his neck and blowing through bright pink nostrils. Twice he circled, then "Trot," Emma commanded and felt her skin prickle at the visual delight of his long smooth stride.

"Good boy, *good* boy," softly she called to him, delighted to see how well he had settled down. "Tomorrow we shall go on a lovely little ride," she cooed on. "Now, canter."

The big gelding bucked, but only once, then he fell into a slow and perfect lope around her.

"Whoa," Emma called, and again Hal obeyed.

After much fondling and praise and treating him to a carrot, Emma rearranged the lunge line and turned him around to work in the other direction. And so they kept at it for the better part of an hour, with time off for rests, for Hal was far from fit and his coat grew quickly damp. "Nerves," Emma muttered, feeling it.

So total was her concentration that she jumped when a voice cried, "Bravo, darling!"

Emma spun around; instantly her sense of

wholeness evaporated, for there, perched on the gate was her grandmother.

"Gee," she said, swallowing, making an effort to smile.

Hal took advantage of her distraction immediately and began to crop the sparse paddock grass; as he did so the line pulled through Emma's fingers. She caught him by the halter, avoiding her grandmother's eye, bewildered by the emotions that swelled in her chest: fright, dread, resentment at Gee for reminding her of the letter in the Music Room.

When she had turned Hal loose in the orchard pasture, she returned to the barnyard gate, coiling the lunge line with acute attention, in order not to look up. When finally she did, Gee was still there, waiting for her, and Emma, approaching, felt her agitation abate, so normal and lighthearted her grandmother looked, so alert, obviously impatient to hear all about Hal.

Why, there's nothing wrong with her, Emma thought, her world reassembling, and she hurried over to babble the story of her morning in the barn. And when they walked briskly up to the house and went in the Music Room door, there was no sign of the letter, so that Emma, with only a little effort, was able to persuade herself that she had imagined the whole matter—or at least grossly exaggerated it.

. . .

After lunch Emma recorded each detail of the morning's work in her journal. Then she caught Mrs. Tiggywinkle, put a halter on her, and climbed onto the broad sway back, startled to discover that her toes almost touched the ground on either side. Using a lead line as reins, she directed the old pony down the lane to fetch the mail.

"Look, Gee, you hit the jackpot." Leaving Mrs. Tig tied to a tree, she joined her grandmother in the garden. "A letter from Cousin Horace, one from Libba, another from Mom, and here's a postcard from Pip, which I've read, and he *is* coming for the Fourth—by the way, Gee, your nails are a sight. Do clean them before your lawyer friend arrives."

Gee sat back on her heels, banged her hands together to clean the dirt from them and, after working absently at her fingernails with the trowel, took the mail. She read quickly through her letters and reported to Emma, "Yes, well, Cousin Horace is coming for the Fourth, too—he'll take the bus with Pip. And Libba and the kids—they'll arrive with Pam. Your Mom says she and Pop will come with the others in August. . . . I'll be glad to see Horace," she mused, half to herself. "He must be—my word, he must be ninety this year. A bit creaky by now, I bet. Lucky thing the guest room's downstairs." She cocked her head. "Here comes Jim."

"Gee, you have the ears of a bat," said Emma.

"Oh, there, I hear it now, down by the brook, but how do you know it's his car?"

"Well, it's three o'clock for one thing, he strikes me as being prompt by nature, and I know he drives a pickup. Besides, there isn't much traffic out here, after all."

A few moments later the sound changed, faded, then increased, and a small blue truck appeared around the bend in the lane. By the time it swung under the maple near the Music Room and came to a stop, Gee and Emma had left the garden and started across the lawn.

Out of the pickup stepped a tall man, thin, with light-colored eyes—were they green, blue, gray? Emma, struck by them, could not decide. They were rimmed by black lashes, and he had very dark, thick, lively hair, which tended to curl around his ears and looked, she thought, as though it needed a determined hand to groom. She was aware of a prickle of hostility at her first sight of the author of that letter.

Gee greeted the lawyer warmly, however, so Emma offered her hand when her grandmother introduced them and found herself almost disarmed by the kindness of his smile.

"Hello, Emma, I've heard a lot about you from your grandmother," he said.

Emma nodded politely, coolly, unwilling quite to capitulate to his obvious good intent. Smoothie, she thought, although smooth was the last thing he looked, she had to admit, seeing him almost blush before he turned to collect his briefcase from the front seat of the truck.

"Come along, Jim, let's get this over with. Em, put the kettle on at four-thirty, will you, and we'll have tea," said Gee, preceding the lawyer into the house. He turned to wave at Emma before following.

Hazel, Emma decided, watching the screen door shut behind them. She shrugged and returned to the garden wall to unhitch Mrs. Tiggywinkle and lead her to the barn.

At five o'clock the three of them sat under the tree-house maple on the edge of the lawn. It was a favorite family spot: The fact that Gee invited Jim Fothergill to have tea there after their meeting was not lost on Emma. Then, when she saw that Gee had brought out the three cups made of her favorite china—china she had been collecting piece by piece for years and seldom used—Emma raised her eyebrows.

Well, well, she thought, he's certainly wormed his way into her heart. But, having left her barnyard in apple-pie order for the night and all its members happy, Emma was in a good mood and thus more disposed to accept Gee's favorable opinion of her new lawyer.

Not sure whether to call him Mr. Fothergill or Jim, Emma simply lifted the pot in his direction. "More tea?"

"Thank you, Emma," he said gravely and held out his cup. The hand was sun-browned, she noticed, with long fingers and deep, well-shaped nails. "These are pretty cups. I've never seen china like this." He turned the pink-and-white saucer over.

"No, there's no trademark," said Gee. "It's worth nothing, really, this china. I saw it for the first time when I sailed to Europe with my father —he was captain of a small liner then. I was in my teens, so it's all of forty years old. The nice thing is that I loved it then and I love it now—so often one's taste changes.

"But it's almost impossible to find. Too old to be in stock anywhere, too new to be considered an antique. I'm glad you like it."

An hour later, when the lawyer stood up to leave, Gee rose, too, and kissed him spontaneously on the cheek.

"You *are* a great help, Jim," she said; and her voice, full of meaning, triggered the alarm in Emma's stomach, instantly replacing her tentative acceptance of Gee's lawyer with distrust.

As he drove down the lane, Gee stood at the crest of the hill, waving him out of sight. "I'm lucky to have found him," she said.

"So you say," Emma answered crossly, collecting the cups and shaking crumbs from the cookie plate onto the grass. The long shadows lying over the lawn and fields, which had so entranced her yesterday, now increased her sense of foreboding. "Who does he think he is, calling you Gee?" Emma heard the edge in her voice and knew she was unreasonable; most people, of all ages, did call Gee that. "I mean, for God's sake, he's not all that much older than Dan."

"A little older. Jim turned thirty-one in May," said Gee.

Oh, well, thought Emma, I guess that does make him old enough.

A silence fell between them. Emma picked up the tea tray and started for the house.

"Emma." Gee's voice was sharp.

Emma turned around. "What?"

"How did you know he called me Gee? He never called me anything the whole time you were here. I even noticed and thought he might feel shy about it. So how did you know he calls me Gee?"

Emma felt her face freeze and then go numb. She grasped the tray so hard that the edge cut into the balls of her thumbs. Staring helplessly at her grandmother, unable to speak, she was overwhelmed, first, by the enormity of her invasion of Gee's privacy, and then by fear at having to confront what she had found out.

In an effort to stave off the billowing pain, she concentrated on studying her shadow, which was beginning to resemble a faceless black figure on stilts.

"You read his letter, then?" Gee's voice was soft, unaccusing.

Emma felt her eyes fill and overflow, two little rillets of hot tears curving round her cheekbones and down either side of her face.

She looked down and nodded, still unable to speak; the tears flowed faster and faster, until finally she sobbed, "Oh, Gee, are you very sick?"

Gee came across the lawn and took the tray from Emma's hands and set it on the grass. Standing straight again, she placed her hands lightly on Emma's shoulders.

"My darling," she said to the bent head. "Yes, I am sick. I did not want anyone to know just yet."

Emma fought for control. Are you going to die? The question hurtled round and round inside her. She could not bring it out, she could not.

At the thought of death, an icy blackness seeped through her and she felt a terrible central despair. At last, from her very core, in a small wet whisper, she drew forth the dreaded words.

"Are you going to die?"

"I do not know," Gee said. With her hand, lightly, she touched the top of Emma's head. "It is possible. I am having treatments. Until we know for sure, Doctor Langdon and I, I want the summer to proceed as always. When—*if*—I cannot manage as usual, then we will discuss when and how to tell the family, and what to do. You and I and Jim, we will decide then."

Emma raised her eyes. "You must never lie to me," she said.

"I won't. I promise," said Gee.

That evening, explaining to Emma that the time with Jim Fothergill had tired her, Gee went to bed early.

"I'll leave the dishes for you," she said, standing in the door to the hall, a cup of tea in her hand. "Please don't worry about my eating"—as she saw Emma glance at her plate—"there are days when I'm just not hungry, and Dr. Langdon says I don't have to force myself. I feel pretty well, darling. I'm just tired, and that happens quite often." She smiled. "I'm glad you know. It's good to be able to talk to you. Good night." She turned and headed for the stairs.

But I don't know much, Emma thought, bleakly, gathering up glass and china and silverware, I don't know why you're sick or when it happened or how long it will last—she veered off that path.

Going to the sink, she scraped Gee's small helping of greens into the compost barrel and rinsed the dishes and drew hot water to wash them.

And you don't talk about it at all, not even about what the lawyer came for, especially not about selling the farm. At the very idea, her eyes filled with tears so that she had to rinse the soap from her hands and fumble for the dish towel to dry her face.

Emma felt a tremendous urge to cry, to give way, to dissolve and vanish in a flood of grief. Perhaps if she did that, poured herself out until nothing was left, someone would come along and put her together again, and this new, clean Emma would know nothing about dying.

Upstairs footsteps made the floorboards creak, water ran in a pipe, a door closed. Gee was going to bed.

Not now, Emma said to herself. Not here. She polished the last fork and laid it in its box. I'll go to the tree house.

The sun was gone, sunk below the hill, but in its wake the sky was iridescent, the twilight strong and vibrant. Colossal, serpentine, slightly pink in the afterglow of the day, the lowest branch of the maple dipped almost to the ground. Emma found the feel of rough bark reassuring as she hauled herself up and made her way along the branch to the tree's great trunk. Mounting the primitive ladder nailed to it, she reached the tree house and climbed inside.

At the sight of its familiar splintery plank walls

43

and floor, waves of nostalgia rippled through her. She spied a shabby stuffed rabbit in a corner. Could it be her old Flopsy? She picked it up, sniffed it. No. Matt's perhaps. Impulsively she kissed it and laid it in her lap.

The tree house seemed a great deal smaller than she remembered. Part of her knew perfectly well that this was simply because she had grown, but she minded anyway. Emma hated change.

Settling herself in one corner, she let the events of the day overtake her. With an almost physical effort of will, she said aloud, "Gee is going to die."

Immediately the blackness that had engulfed her on the lawn returned; despair seized her heart, squeezing it until it hurt. It seemed to stop the flow of blood through her veins, so that her face and fingers grew numb. I will die, too, Emma now knew. Someday I will die, and I am scared.

Now she wished she had not come to the tree house. Here, free to dissolve, she was vulnerable, for there was no one for whom to hold on. She was alone with herself, without escape or pretense, and she could feel her defenses crumbling one by one.

"I can't stand it," she whispered, the breath in her throat hot and unfamiliar, as though it leaked from a big black bag of fear. "I can't stand it," she said again, muffling the words so that she would not scream.

A sudden noiseless pounding overwhelmed her.

44

Oh, God, listen to my heart, it's going to burst. I'm getting out of here.

In a panic she jumped up and reached for the ladder. As she clutched the top rung a splinter pricked her, the sharp little pain bringing her headlong flight to a halt. She sucked her finger, and her eye fell on the stuffed rabbit, fallen from her lap and abandoned on the floor of the tree house; and to her amazement she heard—over the uproar in her chest—her own voice speaking to her.

It said, you can't just let go like that. You are here, now, with Gee. And you must see this through with her.

Slowly but surely the rushing noise subsided, and—still sucking at the splinter—Emma sat down again.

After a while, after the twilight had turned to night, she climbed down from the tree house and walked slowly back across the lawn, the grass cool against the soles of her bare feet.

From the direction of the barn came comforting evening noises: the *throck, thchock, chrock* of horses grazing, a cat courting in the hayloft, the muted bleat of a lamb in search of its dam; but Emma barely heard them.

Like an automaton, she went into the Music Room and through the kitchen and up the stairs to her room. Without turning on her light, not caring where the mouse might be, she undressed and got into bed. Only then did she cry a little, softly, letting the tears slide into her pillow. She cried for her golden summer, lost now, and the last, she felt in her heart of hearts, the last at Bell Brook Farm.

The weather remained light and merry, one perfect day following another as June passed its midpoint. Gee continued to look and act as well as she had on Emma's first morning at the farm; indeed, so hale and serene did her grandmother appear that Emma's gloom dispersed until she began really to believe that Gee would recover and the summer be restored to them.

The barn work took on a rhythm of its own, and Emma filled page after page in her notebook with details of her schedule and occasional private insights of her own. She reported the illness of one of the older lambs, along with its medical history and the treatment prescribed by Doctor Stevens. She logged in two new litters of kittens. Each day's routine chores—feeding, grooming, doctoring, training, cleaning, exercising—were meticulously recorded with observations on various aspects of animal life, Chloe's approaching accouchement in particular. And every afternoon she rode Hal.

Betweentimes she helped Gee with the heavier garden work. They took walks together and drove often to Winslow to do errands or visit friends or shop at the grocery store. Emma swam daily in the pond and usually her grandmother joined her.

Although Gee ate little, she still took an interest in their meals. In the evenings they sat long at the kitchen table after supper, playing backgammon and talking about their day or other members of the family or a movie they'd both liked.

"The girls keep urging me to get a VCR," Gee said one evening. "Dan even offered to buy one for me—imagine, out of his Navy pay—but I don't want one. I love movies as a rule, but there are so many violent ones these days, and I hate them. They affect me."

"You can rent all different kinds, Gee."

"I know. I rented a machine once. It took me forever and a day to choose a movie. Then the phone—which hadn't peeped all day—never stopped ringing. By the time the movie was over, after all those interruptions, it was so late I could hardly drag myself to bed. And then I had to get it back to Winslow before noon the next day, just when I had people turning up for lunch. Thank you very much, but no thanks."

"We play them a lot at home," said Emma.

Gee looked at her sharply. "You miss them? You sure are short on entertainment here."

"Oh, no, Gee, not a bit. It's funny, but it's like leading a whole other life, when I'm here, and

VCRs just aren't part of it."

"Other people your age should be, though."

"Oh, come on, Gee, what with family and visitors coming and going, and there'll be the picnic on the Fourth, not to mention my birthday party. Good grief, I can hardly find enough time in the day for the project."

"Well, I'm glad the Fourth is just around the corner. Pam and Libba and Co. will liven things up for you."

Emma put her hand on her grandmother's arm. "Gee, I do not need livening up, any more than you need a VCR. Thank you very much, but no thanks."

Gee smiled. "Well, I tell you what: For to-night's entertainment let's play the tape and then go to bed."

So Emma put on "We Saw the Sea," and they trilled away to their hearts' content with Fred Astaire's sailors. Even Dumbo joined in at the end with a long mournful howl, which sent Gee and Emma into stitches of laughter and caused old Witch to grimace in her sleep.

In the middle of the second week of Emma's summer, John Lunt and his nephew Eddie appeared with two tractors, a mower, and the tedder, to begin haying. Although the racket they made impinged sharply on the summer tranquility of Bell

Brook Farm, both Gee and Emma enjoyed haying season greatly.

Gee loved to see the landscape change as the tall, lush hay went down and the great south meadow became a geometric tapestry of silver-green windrows, and Emma delighted in watching it being baled and loaded.

"Those hay wagons remind me of the toy wagons made of matchsticks that we had as children," Emma said to Gee one day.

She had come up from the barn after exercising the younger pony and found her grandmother perched on the garden wall, watching John work. Like magic, as the baler passed over the swaths of tedded hay, one perfect cube after another flew up and dropped into the spindly wagon that trailed behind.

"Look at that!" said Emma gleefully, as yet another bale shot up into the air. "I can't get over how accurate John is, aiming them so perfectly, remote-control."

While haying lasted, Emma added to her regular duties the job of helping load the bales into the hayloft. It was a hot and sticky business. Each wagonload was driven to the barn. There John started the power-driven elevator, which leaned against the east end, and stationed Eddie in the loft to receive and arrange the bales. Emma stayed at the foot of the elevator to pass bale after bale from the wagon to the escalating track.

One afternoon Jim Fothergill arrived to talk to Gee. Afterwards, he came down to the barnyard and joined Emma in her work. When the last bales were loaded, they walked back to the house together. Just as Emma was about to go in, she turned back toward Jim, who was opening the door of his pickup.

"Thanks . . . thanks a lot," she said.

So apparent to them both was the lack of a name that the lawyer looked at her with a twinkle. "Jim," he said.

Emma smiled back. "Thanks, Jim," she said.

Because they were blessed with perfect weather, haying was over in a week.

The week before the Fourth, after John and all his equipment left, Gee pronounced her gardens under control for the time being and turned her attention to preparing for the arrival of two of her daughters and their families, and Cousin Horace, and Pip. Although neither she nor Emma mentioned the subject, it was tacitly understood that Gee had no plans at all to ride Hal.

She concentrated first on finishing the mural she had been painting off and on since the middle of the winter. It was in the bathroom she shared with Emma—and soon would have to share also with various babies—and the pots of paint and brushes were beginning to get on her nerves.

Gee's mural was a farm scene, filled with familiar landscapes and animals. For months she had been disturbed by the proportions of the colt over the bathtub: the legs were too long, and she had decided, finally, to get it over with, to paint him out and replace him with more sky and pasture.

"Quite a wrench," she admitted the next morning, as she stood in the tub obliterating the top half of the colt with blue paint. Emma watched from the doorway, a piece of toast in one hand. She liked the long-legged colt and was sorry to see him go.

Gee had drawn him from a snapshot of Chloe's first foal. In her mural he occupied a key position, standing tall—too tall, alas—over the tub, surrounded by lesser inmates of the barn, such as the geese and the sheep, two barn cats playing with a ball of blue yarn, and a mourning dove, all framed by the barn doorway. On the wall over the sink was the house and maple trees, with the hill behind leading up to the ten-acre lot, which almost touched the ceiling; while above the toilet Gee had persuaded a friend to cut a half-circle out of the plaster board, install a light bulb, and cover it with orange Plexiglas, around which she had painted sky above and rolling hillsides below. Now, when she flipped the switch by the door, there was a fair rendering of the sun rising over the hills across the valley.

With a final swoosh of her brush, the last of the colt disappeared.

"He was just too dominant—this way there'll be more depth to the room," she said. "And I won't feel so breathed upon while bathing."

"Perhaps," Emma agreed reluctantly. She licked her fingers one by one. Gee was a tyrant about crumbs. "By the way, Gee, my mouse is gone. I don't hear any of them anymore."

A few deft strokes and the colt's smudge became a late spring sky and rich spring grass.

"That's because it's summer. They'll be back at the first hint of winter, never fear." And a shadow crossed Gee's face.

The mural was finished.

Gee stepped carefully out of the tub and began to collect all her painting paraphernalia. "Thank goodness Bertha can give us a hand with the cleaning and making up all those beds," she said. Then she turned to Emma and looked her in the eye. "It's no use pretending I can do it all myself anymore. I promised not to lie to you."

She pushed the paint cans and drop cloth to the rear of the bathroom closet and started for the door with the two dirty brushes. As she passed, Gee laid her hand on top of Emma's head and said, "Come on, pumpkin. Jim's coming for supper. Come help me decide what to have, before you go back to work."

At Gee's urging Emma stayed out of the house most of the day.

"Bertha is a marvel—she not only works twice as hard as I ever did, she thinks twice as fast. You'd only be in the way, honey."

So, after her usual training session with Hal and a long, ambling, sentimental ride on Mrs. Tiggywinkle; after lungeing the younger pony for half an hour to keep him fit for Gee's middle-aged grandchildren—the six-, seven-, and eight-year-olds who would be turning up throughout the summer—she spent the time before evening chores in the hayloft writing in her journal.

July 1. Today Gee admitted she was sick— it was the first time since the night after I got here. I guess it was dumb of me to think she was getting better and better. I can see for myself that she moves slower than she used to, and she's thinner and she still hardly eats, but otherwise she seemed fine. How much was I fooling myself? Did I really think I was working Hal for her? That we'd ride together this summer? Part of me did. Part of me still thinks she'll be OK. Why did she have to spoil it all by admitting out loud she couldn't work the way she used to? Emma paused. *I know I made her promise not*

to lie, but still—she said herself that Dr. Lang-
don didn't know whether she was going to d—
get worse or better. Actually, all she said today
was that she needed help, that's not so bad.

This afternoon Hal went better than ever. He
is moving like a star—every gait—and he loves
to jump. After ring work I took him round the
edge of the big meadow, over the little jump
course I made when John finished haying—(she
flipped back a few pages to see what the date
had been)—*and it was heaven. The two of us*
move as one. It's like gliding, or how I think it
would be to glide, when we get going around
that course. You have to pay attention every
single second to stay in tune with Hal, to stay in
control of him, but you have to let go and be
part of him, too. Today really was heaven.

She tucked her pen inside the journal and closed
it. Recalling and writing about her work with Hal
had restored her serenity. She stood up, scratched
where the hay made her itch and breathed deeply
of the heady, sweet smell in the newly filled loft.

Mary Jo doesn't know what she's missing, she
thought, picturing her best friend working in a
fish cannery for the summer in order to be near her
boyfriend. Emma sighed contentedly and started
down the ladder to begin evening chores.

. . .

Jim had already arrived when Emma finished in the barn. She saw the little blue pickup drawn up by the Music Room door. Entering the house, Emma could tell right away that Bertha Simmons had been there: Everything shone with a special polished look and the air smelled of wax and pine soap and ironing. It smelled, too, of one of Gee's specialities, a chicken stew laced with brandy, mint, and ginger, and Emma noticed that her grandmother had set the dining room table. Except for special occasions—such as when Cousin Horace or old friends from the city came to visit Gee—they usually only ate in the dining room if there were to be more than eight to a sitting. The kitchen was really the heart of Bell Brook Farm.

Gee came into the kitchen now, dressed in the long caftan that she often changed into for supper. It became her; she looked well, even—Emma thought to her surprise—quite beautiful.

"Run change, pumpkin. Jim and I are drinking wine in the sitting room. I'm just going to put the rice on, then we'll eat. Look—I set the dining-room table"—she chuckled—"to practice for Cousin Horace and the descending hordes."

But Emma could tell Gee was enjoying doing it for the lawyer, and she grinned, happy to see the old familiar spark of energy.

When it grew dark enough, over dessert, Gee lit the four candles. In the glow they shed, the faces around the table took on a soft ethereal look. Gee's lines disappeared, Emma noticed, and Jim looked almost as young as Pip, and his kind hazel eyes darkened and shone with a quiet, merry gravity.

For a while they continued to chat about one thing and another going on around the countryside —the Winslow Fair, in August, the roast-beef supper at the church in Doe's Crossing, Mrs. Archer's Fourth of July picnic on Saturday.

"Are you going?" Emma asked Jim, out of politeness.

The lawyer turned to her. "Yes. It will be my first time. When I moved to Winslow last year I didn't really get to know Mrs. Archer until after the picnic. What should I expect? Do tell me, Emma."

"Well," said Emma, digging into her rhubarb pie. "First of all, don't dress up. On the other hand, don't be too sloppy. Mrs. Archer is an old, old-fashioned lady. No tie, but no bare feet, either." She bent to look under the table before returning to her pie. "What you're wearing now would be okay. But sneakers are better than shoes, for the games. There's just the usual cookout food—hamburgers and hot dogs and all. A bonfire. Singing. Usually someone plays the guitar and Lettie Reynolds always brings her bugle. After supper everyone plays games—baseball, Frisbee; the little ones play tag. It's all ages. I bet you'll find people your age—oh, but of course, my aunts Libba and Pam will introduce you to their friends. The best part is the sparklers, when it gets dark enough. . . ."

Suddenly Emma realized she had prattled on for quite a long time. She raised her eyes from her plate and found Jim's fixed upon her. He smiled quickly, looked down at his pie, and took up his fork. "Yes? And the sparklers?"

In the sitting room after supper Gee and Jim sipped coffee and Emma curled up in her favorite chair, one elbow on its arm, her chin in one hand, and listened to their desultory conversation. It was only 9:30 but she felt deliciously relaxed and sleepy. Vaguely, she was aware that Gee had set down her cup and turned to her.

"Now, darling, would you like to be caught up on what Jim and I have been meeting about these past weeks?"

Emma froze. No! she shouted inside. "Yes," she said meekly, unfolding herself and sitting up a little.

"Well, as you must remember from that letter" —Emma dropped her eyes—"and as I know you must have gathered from all our telephone conversations, I have been really very anxious about the future of Bell Brook Farm, that is, if things don't turn out well for me. . . ."

When Gee fell silent for a moment, Emma looked up again.

"I'll be having some tests next week—after the Fourth. They should tell us quite a lot."

Emma regarded her unflinchingly.

"Now, the good news is that Jim thinks he may be able to figure out a way to keep the farm in the family, no matter what."

Meaning if you die, Emma thought, suddenly and fiercely. Why don't you just say it?

"That is, if I die soon," Gee went on; and Emma, caught off guard, felt her rage erupt. "You can't die, you have no *right* to die," she stormed. "It is unthinkable, *unforgivable*."

"This sounds cold-blooded, even to me." Gee was still talking, and Emma forced herself to listen. "But I thought it best to speak of it, partly because I take my promises seriously, as you know, and it's been a while since we've talked about all this"— here Emma, watching her grandmother, realized that Gee had guessed her thoughts and was trying to placate her—"and partly, Emma, because should things take a turn for the worse, it appears they will move fairly rapidly. Jim and you and I will be together a good deal, making decisions, arrangements . . . that is, assuming you want to finish the summer here?"

The really violent anger that had seized Emma evaporated; she sat bolt upright.

"*What!* What are you saying—? Oh, Gee—" A stinging assailed her eyes and the bridge of her nose. I will not cry in front of him, she said to herself through clenched teeth. She paused and breathed in to collect herself. "Gee, no matter what, no matter *what*, I want to be here, with you, for the whole summer."

Emma planned to go on, to lighten her tone by adding, "Besides, *you promised* me a sixteenth birthday party," but, not wanting to falter in front of Jim and not quite trusting her voice, she held her tongue.

And Jim began to speak. "Gee and I are working on a disposition of Bell Brook Farm which we have hopes will pass probate court; she knows how much you care and thought you should know about it from the start, and I agree." Emma found it easy to listen to his slightly twanging voice and felt the weight of her own emotions lighten. "I'll go over it with you whenever you want—basically, it just puts the place on hold for a while, gives the family plenty of time, in the event of her death, without invading the rest of her assets—" He broke off with a snort. "What *language!* Anyway I feel good about the three of us knowing how things stand, and I'm sure you do, too, from what Gee tells me. . . . Now, Gee, you just pass those tests with flying colors and we can forget the whole business." He stood up, put his cup on the tray.

"I'd better go along. Thank you for a delicious dinner."

They followed him through the house to the Music Room, where he had left his briefcase.

"What a night!" Gee exclaimed at the window. "Look. The moon's nearly full."

"Yes," said Jim. "It'll be full the night of the picnic."

"Oh, I hope and pray the weather holds." Emma, standing in the doorway, gazed up at the sky. "Even though the sparklers don't sparkle so much, there's nothing like a full moon on the Fourth of July. Maybe it'll even bring on Chloe's foal."

Jim laughed. "Maybe it will indeed. My mother always said it brought me on! Good night. Thank you both again for the dinner, for the whole evening."

Ducking, he got into the pickup and drove off down the lane.

A little later, in her bed, as Emma thought over the scene in the sitting room, it became clear to her that Gee did not want to take her by surprise; that, while her grandmother did not wish to discuss her threatened health with anyone—even her own children, as yet—she nonetheless wanted to include Emma in the reality of the situation. If Gee failed those tests next week, Emma now fully realized, she would want to keep every aspect of life at Bell Brook Farm unchanged for as long as possible.

Gee needed an ally in the family, and she had designated Emma.

Jim was right, she decided. I think I feel better, knowing how things stand.

Pam and Libba arrived. They drove up from Boston with all their children on the Thursday before the holiday weekend.

Emma looked into the station wagon and groaned. "God, you two, just *look* at this stuff—does it go *everywhere* with you?"

"You just wait, Em," said Libba. "Just one small baby will do it, and we've got quite a little army with us."

Emma opened the tailgate and began to unload the car, starting with Libba's gear, which was packed in the rear. Out came four-year-old George's duffel bag, his baby brother's king-sized box of plastic diapers, George's potty chair, the baby's folding bed, a bundle of dirty clothes, five brown paper bags, a carton filled with bottles, nipples, and plastic tops, George's wooden train, bridge, station, and passengers—from which he was seldom if ever parted—Libba's suitcase, her junk bag (full of junk), her raincoat, her handbag, her knitting bag and—after a frantic search that involved disemboweling every piece of luggage— the baby's nunny, a disgusting strip of napless blanket, encrusted with unthinkable substances, without which the baby would neither sleep nor eat.

Pam was simpler. As of now she only had two quite grown-up boys: Jason, seven-and-a-half, and Matthew, five. Nonetheless, it took the better part of an hour to get everything settled in the right rooms.

When they all gathered at the kitchen table for tea later that afternoon, Emma regarded Pam's stomach.

"Does it move much?" she asked.

"I'll say. It wakes me up every morning. Hey, it's moving now, want to feel?"

She took Emma's hand and placed it on her high, round belly.

"Nothing's happen—Oh! Pam! Pam! It's moving," Emma cried, her eyes shining. She poked the baby gently. "Do it again," she said.

Pam laughed. "It's got a mind of its own, Em."

"'It,'" said Gee. "'It.' I wonder what 'it' will be. Do you feel any different this time, Pammy?"

"Yes and no. I'm carrying it differently from the boys, and I had a *passion* for peanut butter the first couple of months. But I guess that doesn't mean much."

"So you think it *might* be a girl?" asked Emma. "We sure could use a girl, with all these boys."

Libba, shelling Gee's first crop of peas, said, "Well, it's bound to be one or the other. We'll know in October."

Sounds of strife came from the lawn, followed by a baby's wail. Emma jumped up.

"I'll go," she said and dashed out the door, unable to bear the look of wistful hope on Gee's face at the thought that Pam might have a girl in October.

That evening Emma noticed that Gee made a valiant effort to eat her supper. Later, when she cleared the plates after the others moved into the Music Room, she discovered, however, that her grandmother had hidden most of her chop under a lettuce leaf. Standing at the kitchen sink, Emma marveled that the aunts had not remarked on their mother's thinness, especially as they had not seen her for several weeks.

Just then, Pam came into the kitchen to help. "Here, Em, I'll dry," she said, leaning back against the drainboard and taking a cluster of knives and forks in one hand and a dish towel in the other. "How's the summer going?"

"Great, Pam. I love it here, you know, and I love the so-called work."

"Ma says she doesn't know what she'd do without you." Pam laid the silverware on the table and took up another handful. "Do you think she feels well? She looks awfully thin to me. Thin, and sort of . . . otherworldly." Pam snorted. "Funny word. It just popped into my head."

So great was Emma's longing to confide in Pam, her favorite aunt, that she had to turn away and busy herself looking for a clean dish towel in the drawer behind her in order to hang on to her promise to Gee. *I wish Pip were here. Then she'd have told us both. Maybe he'll guess anyway. Pip doesn't miss much.*

"Perhaps it's just that she's getting older. Ma's always said people age in fits and starts. Still . . . something's different. What do you think, Em?"

Emma almost let go. Later, she wondered whether she would have blurted out the whole story to Pam had not the sailors' charming voices wafted into the kitchen from the Music Room.

"Oh, good," said Pam. "She's put it on. She was *so* tickled by that tape, Em. Come on, let's go join them."

The next evening, taking Emma with her, Libba went to fetch Pip and Cousin Horace in Winslow. Emma was not sure how she felt about the gathering crowd at Bell Brook Farm. At first she had looked forward to the influx of clan and the reassuring familiarity of the scene. But this time everything was different. On the one hand it was a welcome relief to have so many distractions; on the other, she felt as though she were leading a double life.

"Whew," said Libba. "Peace and quiet. Nice to get away from the little darlings for a bit. What a madhouse it'll be over your birthday, when the whole gang's here. Just think, Em, sweet sixteen. From my advanced years"—Libba was twenty-eight—"I look back on sixteen as the Threshold of Life."

She took her eyes off the road long enough to squeeze Emma's knee and give her a comical Rabelaisian leer. "What'll we do tomorrow when the husbands arrive?"

"Well, it'll be late when they get here and Mrs. Archer's is Saturday evening. How about a picnic at White Rock on Sunday?" said Emma. "The walkers can walk up, Pip and I can ride, and Gee and Cousin Horace and the babies and Matt can go in the jeep. . . ."

"How restful," said Libba.

"And then we can swim at Twenty-Foot on the way home."

"Rob loves Twenty-Foot," Libba said, smiling at the memory of the first time she had shown her husband the sylvan river pool. Then, out of the blue: "Now, what's going on with Ma? Something's missing, or added. Something's different anyway. I can't put my finger on it. Any ideas?"

Oh, God, thought Emma, now Libba. "She's off her feed, that's all. Otherwise everything's going fine, just like always—"

" 'As,' " they said in unison and giggled.

"Okay, glamorous, cosmopolitan Winslow Station, here we come," said Libba, braking in front of the tatterdemalion little bus depot.

The bus was actually on time. Cousin Horace

crept off it cautiously, using his cane to feel his way down the steps and onto Libba's proffered arm. Once grounded, however, he resumed his spry, birdlike gait.

"Pip's at the back," he said, offering a smooth, papery cheek to Emma. "We couldn't sit together. Never mind, we'll catch up at the farm." Pip and Cousin Horace were old friends, given to spirited arguments and crafty, unorthodox games of croquet.

Then, there was Pip, standing like an avatar in the doorway of the bus. He threw his duffel bag ahead of him and jumped down, and Emma's heart jerked to think how nearly they had lost him five years ago. That awesome summer Pip hovered, gray and sweating, on the edge of death for hours while Emma and Gee and Doctor Langdon yearned over him, willing him to come back to them. Now look at him, she thought to herself, regarding her brother's tan and radiant face as he approached.

"God, it's good to be back," he said, cuffing her gently with the knuckles of one hand. "Hi, Em. Come on, Lib, let's *go*."

At seven o'clock on the morning of the Fourth of July, Emma burst through the Music Room door and up the step into the kitchen.

"Gee!" she panted. "Gee, Chloe's acting funny. When I went down to feed, she was wandering around with a faraway look in her eye and she's all swollen and dripping behind."

Gee, at the sink, turned around with a smile. "Well, well, well. Good old Chloe; right on the button. Keep your voice down, honey. Everyone else is still asleep."

"Oh, Gee, come look at her, do. I've put her in the foaling stall with lots of hay and a big bucket of water. What else?" Eyes popping, breathless, Emma clasped her hands together. "Come on, Gee, come see."

So Gee laid down her sponge and followed Emma down to the barn.

Entering the cool, dark lower level, they were greeted by a Brandenburg concerto. Light and flawless, the notes from the radio next to the foaling stall filled the barn.

"Well, that's a nice way to start labor," said Gee cheerfully. "I remember when I had Dan I listened to the *Marriage of Figaro* all the way through to act four, scene one; then just when Barbarina tells Figaro she has lost the pin, Dan arrived and I was too busy to hear the end. Oh, Chloe, my word, you do look ready," she said, peering into the stall. "As you said, Em, she looks as though she were living in another world."

Gee reached up to stroke the lovely gray nose, but Chloe pulled away restlessly and moved to the far end of her luxurious quarters.

"Wait till I tell Jim—I just know it's because of

the moon! *When* do you think it will come?"
Emma was quite beside herself with excitement.
She felt like a little girl whose dreams are about
to come true. Always she had wanted to see a
newborn foal, and especially to be there when it
came, and, now, despite all her plans and prep-
arations, she could hardly believe it was actually
happening.

"Heavens, Em, I don't know. I'll tell you one
thing, though. She'll try to have it when you're not
looking. Mares are like that. So if you don't want
to miss it, and if you don't want to upset Chloe,
you'd better be prepared to spend an awful lot of
time peeking—there, there's a crack you can see
through. Go in with the sheep and stay *still* and
watch her through that crack, when you see her
time is near."

"What if she has trouble? Won't you be here,
too?"

"If she has trouble, you can fetch me, and I'll
call Dr. Stevens, but otherwise you're in charge
down here. I have a houseful up there."

Gee ran her hand lightly over Emma's brown
head and smiled.

She looks well today, Emma thought, unable to
break herself of reading her grandmother every
morning. Maybe it's just the dark barn, hiding
those lines, but her voice sounds so good and strong.

"You don't think she'll have it before breakfast,

do you?" Emma asked, thinking wistfully of bacon and eggs.

"I'll make no promises, pumpkin. You'll have to take that risk on your own. All I'll say is that they usually foal in the evening, because they know they'll be alone, but you never know for sure."

Emma looked over the stall gate at the mare. Seeming quite her old self, chewing her hay stolidly, Chloe looked back at her.

"No," Emma said. "I'll stay. Please ask Pip to bring me something to eat when he gets up."

"Okay, honey. By the way, be sure not to go near her until she stands up when it's all over. You don't want her on her feet right away or the cord will break too soon."

After Gee left, Emma finished her chores, tidying the barn with extra care to use up time, even dusting the shelves in the tack room. From time to time she passed by the foaling stall and, pretending indifference, glanced briefly in; each time Chloe seemed less likely to deliver her foal that day. She stood gazing out the window, obviously wishing she were out in the pasture with the other horses, eating good green grass.

Never mind, Emma said to herself, trying to ignore her rumbling stomach, it's bound to come sometime.

An hour or so later Pip appeared bearing a fried-egg sandwich and a jar of orange juice.

"Is that *all?*" Emma asked, cranky with hunger.

"All?" repeated Pip, deliberately pompous. "My dear girl, there are people in this world who would go down on their knees—"

"Oh, shut up, Pip, I know all about that, but none of them're here in this barn."

She grabbed the sandwich and wolfed it down.

"Do me a favor," she said, unscrewing the top of the jar, her spirits instantly improved after refueling. "Please, Pip. Please get me my book. It's on my bed. And—" she paused, considering. "If I tell you where to find my journal, will you promise to bring it to me without looking inside?"

"My dear child," said Pip, continuing his tiresome role, "perish the thought."

Reading and writing helped, but it was a long, long day. Emma wondered if it would ever end and whether Chloe might not have fooled them all with a false pregnancy, and what she would decide to do when it came time for Mrs. Archer's picnic. Everybody up at the house was going, even the babies, and Emma hated to think of missing it.

The straw in the sheep pen was scratchy and damp and reeked of manure, the sandwich Pip brought to her for lunch was bologna—her least favorite—and she finished her book at a quarter to three. When the ball-point pen ran out of ink at half-past four, she laid aside her journal, sighed, and looked for perhaps the 150th time through the crack.

"I don't believe it," she whispered. "How did I not hear her?"

Chloe was lying down.

Silent as a cat, Emma spun onto her hands and knees and pressed her face to the crack in the wall.

From under the mare's tail protruded a white sac, rather like a balloon, Emma marveled, watching it grow. Chloe heaved herself, grunting, to her feet. She took a step or two, breathing fast, and sank back down flat on her side in the shavings.

Sweat began to break out on her now, darkening her coat, and she raised her head time and again to look round at her flanks. Once more she struggled to her feet, and the sac ruptured, letting loose a little flood of water. Sweating heavily and grunting, nosing her flanks, Chloe circled the stall twice and then went down. Now she began to push.

From her perfect hidden vantage point Emma watched Chloe's sides heaving as the mare strained to deliver her foal. For perhaps five minutes she labored, grunting loudly with effort and sweating. To Emma it seemed much longer, and she began to worry that the mare needed help and to wonder how ever they could get Dr. Stevens there in time to help Chloe through her travail.

But then—wonder of wonders—two small hooves appeared, covered in jelly, and—above them a moment later—a nose. Emma held her breath.

So this is what it's all about, she thought, torn between revlusion and a kind of rapture. Was it like this for Minnie Rockenheimer? . . . Will it be like for Pam? . . . and *me?*

Chloe heaved, her sides shuddering with the effort, and out slipped the foal. Wet, knobby, ugly, perfect, it lay flat in the bedding Emma had prepared for it, still joined to its mother by a thick, white, ropey cord. Emma almost forgot to let out her breath.

Trembling slightly, she sat back on her haunches and rubbed the palms of her hands, which were numb from her weight. Then, hearing sounds next door, she returned to her spy hole.

Chloe was struggling to her feet. As she did so, the cord broke, releasing a fair amount of blood; and soon after, the foal, still wet-dark and matted, made its first effort to stand. Again and again it tried, stretching out its outlandishly long forelegs, then sliding sideways back into the shavings. Chloe prodded it constantly with her nose, urging it on, until finally, trembling and lurching from side to side, the foal stood on all four feet.

Emma could bear it no longer. She got up and went round quietly to the stall gate and looked in at the mother and foal.

"Bless you, Chloe, oh, God bless you," she

whispered and then turned and ran lightly down the aisle between the stalls and out into the late afternoon sunshine. Once out of the barn, she began to yell.

"*Foal!*" she called up to the house, but no one heard.

"*Foal! Foal! Foal!*" she shouted, running as fast as she could up the lane.

Heads appeared in windows, out onto the lawn ran Pam and Libba and Pip, babies and toddlers looked up from the sandbox near the garden wall, and Gee came to the Music Room door.

"*Foal*," gasped Emma, arriving at the edge of the lawn. "Oh, Gee, it has come."

And she sank down, breathless, onto the grass, her face flushed, grinning, the eyes nearly hidden behind the high brown cheekbones.

"Hurry, Gee, I don't want to miss the after-birth."

Gee came down the steps. "Oh, Em, how thrilling," she called, hurrying across the lawn. "What is it? A boy or a girl?"

Emma's face fell. "I forgot to look," she said.

It was a colt. Immediately, Emma named him Yankee Doodle.

"Well, this certainly seems to be a year for boys," said Gee. "Let's hope Pam has a girl—your generation's a bit lopsided, though I suppose I'm no one to talk."

Chloe had delivered the placenta. The sight of it made Emma feel distinctly queasy, but she forced herself to shovel it up to show Gee she was able to manage every aspect of her job.

By the time they returned to the house, trailed by all who had come to view the foal, Pam and Libba were organizing the seating in Gee's station wagon in order to go to the picnic. Emma ran into the house to change her clothes.

"Don't you think we'd better take two cars?" she heard Gee ask doubtfully, "seeing what a crowd we are?"

"Come on, Ma," said Libba. "We can do it—"

Emma smiled and moved nearer her window as she pulled on a clean pair of khakis.

"It's more fun to go together," Libba went on. "And you know how Mrs. Archer hates too many cars messing up her field. . . . Now, Cousin Horace, in you go—here, take this baby on your lap. Rob, you here next to them. . . ."

Gee began to laugh. "We'll look like the car in the circus."

But one way or another in they squashed, Emma and Pip way in the back, holding Pam's Matt and Libba's George on their laps.

"Whew, some load," Gee said, craning her neck to see around all the bodies. She let out the clutch and coasted down the lane. "Amazing what a difference the extra weight makes," she said

74

half to herself as she negotiated the hairpin turn onto the town road.

"Oh, no, Ma, come on, none of your tricks. We're late as it is," said Pam nervously.

From time to time, as they all well knew, Gee liked to see how far she could get her car to coast on the way to Doe's Crossing before having to throw it into gear. As a rule, the best she could do was 4.1 miles.

Although they were now on the main road to the village, it was, like all the others in the area, a dirt one, less than twice as wide as the lane to the house, and it wound its way past farms, back and forth over Bell Brook, mostly downhill, sometimes level, with two slight rises near the end.

"I bet with this load we can make it past the hump at Orwell's Mill," she said thoughtfully. "And it's just the right time of day for traffic—we won't have to slow up for cars. . . ."

"Yeah, Gee, go for it," Pip called from the back.

So Gee left the car in neutral and set the odometer, and they began to glide down the road through maples and birches, following Bell Brook all the way.

"Ma, come on, slow down for the turn," Pam pleaded from the backseat. Her husband, Harry, laid his hand on her arm. "Honey . . ."

"Remember the time you took the turn into your lane too fast, Gee, and the door flew open and the baby almost rolled out—which baby was it? George, I think. Anyway, it's just lucky Matt grabbed him," said Pip.

"I never should have told you about that one little time—"

Matt took his thumb out of his mouth and, squirming with delight, interrupted his grandmother. "Two times, Gee, it happened two times, one day after the other," he said and returned his thumb to his mouth.

"Twice!" said Pam. "Ma, really!"

"Honey," said Harry with a laugh.

Gee colored. "Come now, Matt, the second time wasn't even close."

She braked gently, slowing the car just enough to execute a sharp turn to the left, and, once on the open straightaway that followed, where the road flattened out, immediately took her foot off the pedal. Libba's Rob opened his mouth, closed it again and turned his head to stare sideways out the window next to him.

This was a tricky stretch to navigate. Too level to maintain momentum for long, it also had washboard patches, which further slowed their progress and threw up clouds of dust, forcing them to close all the windows.

Gee and all her passengers found themselves perched on the edges of their seats to help keep the car moving. Just as it must surely roll to a stop, the descent began again and they picked up speed.

"I *never* believe we'll make that bit," said Gee.

At the first of a series of blind curves, she sat up very straight and grasped the wheel more firmly.

"When I'm alone, I can make this first bend without braking, but—"

"But now you're *not* alone," Pam shouted, clutching her big belly and wrapping the seat belt more tightly around it.

"Honey," said Harry.

"—but now, as I was about to point out, the extra weight gives us enough speed so I'll have to use the brakes—my dear child, I've been doing this since long before you were born."

Gently she tapped the pedal. Hugging the right-hand side of the road, the car careened smoothly round the deep bend, whizzed soundlessly past a small red farmhouse with two dogs and a cat watching stonily from the front porch, and entered an even sharper curve over the brook, which ran its merry way several feet below the road. The old wooden bridge crackled smartly as they crossed it.

Beyond, the road narrowed a bit, but it was straight, the angle of descent eased, and the visibility was good. They rolled along smoothly for quite a way, swaying gently in the shallow curves, raising less dust, and as they neared Orwell's Mill even Pam and Libba caught the spirit of the game. In the front seat, Cousin Horace chuckled helplessly.

"Three point six miles," said Gee. "Here comes the first hump."

Imperceptibly the road had flattened and they lost headway. Ahead on the left was a large farm with a yellow house and large yellow barns. Milking over, men passed to and fro in the barnyard, getting set to quit for the evening. Opposite the house lay the brow of the road, indicating the top of a slight rise; beyond, the road dipped and meandered, with the brook, through a long meadow.

Gee glanced at the speedometer. "Seven, six, five miles an hour," she muttered through gritted teeth. "I hate this part. It's so *embarrassing*. I don't know these people well—they just moved in last year and I haven't called on them yet, and there always seems to be someone about, watching—my word, look at that crew now. Let's pretend we don't see them."

The farmhands stood waiting expectantly for the car to come to a full stop, but it rolled slowly past them, jammed to the gills with people of all ages, all leaning forward tensely, even the babies, eyes glued to the road. Inch by inch the car made the brow, hung on it, and glided slowly down the far side.

"Whew," said Gee. "Okay. That makes 3.8. I would have thought we'd take that faster this evening."

"Me too, Georgia, me too," said Cousin Horace, wiping his eyes.

Pam glanced at her watch. "Ma, we're supposed to *be* there by six. Can't we quit now?"

Pam's husband patted her arm.

"Sh—look: four miles. Here comes the second hump. See—we're moving right along. I knew this load would do it. Fourteen miles per hour. . . ." The road began to rise again. "Twelve, ten, eight, seven—uh-oh."

Mr. Orwell came out of his mill and stood at the side of the road.

"Swing her to the right a little, Gee," he roared, waving his cap as though to blow the car forward. They were barely moving. "No, no. That's enough —straighten the wheels now. By Gawd, I do believe you've got it this time, Gee."

His brown old face wreathed in smiles, he strolled along beside them. As the car moved from a near standstill, he reached in and patted Gee's shoulder.

"Goin' to the picnic, are you? Can't make it this year. . . . Drive carefully, now. Hi, Pam, hi, Libba —and there's Pip way back there—"

Gee beamed at him. "We made it, Chuck! That's only the third time I can remember doing that in my whole life! Four point *seven* miles!"

"My God, Ma," said Pam.

Her husband laughed. "Honey," he said.

79

The road began its last descent to Doe's Crossing, and the station wagon picked up speed.

"Good-bye, Mr. Orwell," shouted Pip, waving furiously at the rear window.

Then they were on the hard-top and Gee put the car in gear.

By the time they arrived at Mrs. Archer's picnic, a goodly number of people of all ages had gathered on her hilltop. Emma spotted Jim Fothergill standing with a couple she remembered from past years. He waved and came over to the car, and she told him about the arrival of the foal. He was so interested that it was several moments before Gee introduced him to Pam and Libba and the husbands.

Pip and Emma took off into the little crowd to look for their old friend, Joey Perry. When they found him, the three of them moved a little apart and sat down on an old stone wall. The boys took turns talking about the past year and their summer jobs, and Emma listened, wholly relaxed, still bemused by her long day of suspense and fulfillment. From time to time Joey tried to draw her into the conversation, but for the most part she was content to gaze across the Connecticut River at the blue hills of New Hampshire, dreamily watching them turn from blue to heather to purple as the sun slowly set behind Mrs. Archer's hill.

It'll be some time before it's dark enough for the

sparklers, she mused; and by then the moon will have started up.

"Hey, Em," Pip nudged her. "They're starting the baseball. Joey and I want to play."

"Yeah, come on, Em. We can play outfield together," said Joey.

But Emma, suddenly hungry, decided to eat first. She joined the knot of people waiting for food and found herself next to Lettie Reynolds in the line.

"Are you going to announce the sparklers with your bugle?" Emma asked her.

"Of course," answered Lettie, and added, with a little laugh, "You know nothing ever changes at these picnics."

Emma did know. That was really why she loved them. Out of the tail of her eye she saw Jim approaching the food table.

"Emma, you want to ride with me this summer?" Lettie was asking. "My mother told me your grandmother lets you use her big chestnut. I'm working on a young thoroughbred this summer, and I'd love to have your company."

Emma's heart swelled. What a lovely invitation. She'd always liked Lettie and looked up to her, Lettie being four or five years older. What fun they would have, but—

"Oh, Lettie, I'd love to, and maybe we can, after next week." (After we get the results of Gee's tests; I won't—I can't—plan anything until then.)

"OK, I'll call you," said the young woman and, catching sight of her boyfriend, moved away.

Emma felt depressed and anxious that Lettie might have taken her answer as a rebuff. When she found it was her turn at the grill, she was no longer hungry and was about to turn away when Jim's voice said, "Two hamburgers, please, and two hot dogs."

He collected them on a paper plate, added globs of relish to one, ketchup to another, and said to Emma, "I don't know how you like them, but we can sort that out. Let's eat."

They sat near the bonfire and Emma found she was hungry, after all. She polished off one hamburger and one hot dog and when she had finished, she noticed that Jim had eaten only the hamburger and that the other hot dog lay, rather soggily, on the plate. She looked at it.

"It must be kind of a strain for you, with the aunts home, not knowing, and you all being so close. I wish I could help."

Emma felt a rush of gratitude. He really was quite nice, after all; she could see why Gee liked him so much.

"Thanks, Jim. It *is* hard. I almost broke down and told Pam. In fact, if Gee hadn't put on an old sailors' song she likes, which made us stop talking, I might have done it." Brows knit, she reflected for a moment. "Actually, don't worry, I really don't think I would have."

"I'm not a bit worried."

Emma looked at the hot dog again.

"Go on, eat it, Em. I'd already had one before, anyway."

So Emma thanked him and ate the hot dog.

"Jim!" called Libba. "Jim! Come on, we need a new pitcher!"

They got up and parted, Jim to the baseball game, and Emma to join a group of singers gathered around Melissa Perry, who had brought her guitar.

When the last trace of sunlight left the sky and only the rim of the moon could be seen in the east, darkness covered Mrs. Archer's hillside.

The sparklers were wonderful.

PART TWO

Pam and Libba and their families left early the morning after the long Fourth of July weekend, but Pip and Cousin Horace stayed on for two more days. Far into the night they continued a running discussion on Eastern mysticism versus Western science, the new physics, reincarnation—none of which interested Emma at all. She did enjoy watching them play their Machiavellian games of croquet, however. Cousin Horace, for all his years, wielded an expert mallet, and he took great delight in knocking Pip's ball down the lane to the barn.

"You cheated! You cheated! I saw you!" yelled Pip. "Pick my ball up, Emma, and bring it right back up here!"

Emma was on her way to the house; she stopped and squinted questioningly at Cousin Horace, who was doubled up with laughter on the lawn.

"That's just it, young feller, you *didn't* see me. You were too busy figuring how to sneak your ball through the wicket while I was playing. My point. You may leave Pip's ball where it is, Emma."

In the afternoons Cousin Horace lay in one of

the old canvas lawn chairs in the garden, watching Gee as she sat at the edge of the beds, turning and turning the earth with her trowel. Emma wondered what they talked about or if they talked at all.

Whenever she joined them, Cousin Horace and Gee seemed to be wrapped in a soft veil of silence; from time to time one of them murmured a few words—often, Emma found, they were reciting poetry to each other. Gee looked happy and peaceful, there in her garden, rested after the strenuous weekend. So visible was the bond of affection between them that Emma wondered if Gee had told Cousin Horace her secret.

But no, I can read her too well now. I'd know, she decided. Gee hasn't told him a thing. They have a special wavelength, that's all; they are devoted to each other.

The night before Pip and Cousin Horace were to leave, the four of them went out to the garden after dinner to sit and watch the moon rise. The night was still and immensely bright. From the pond, through the soft summer air, came the sound of bullfrogs, and in the stubble of the hayfield crickets chirped. There was no sign of the moon as yet, but the stars seemed almost to shout their light into the boundless sky.

As they made their way down the stone steps into the walled garden, it was as though they entered an enchanted and aromatic embrace. Without speaking, they paused, and Emma sensed that the moment held them all, equally, spellbound.

"God, this place," Pip groaned, finally, and they moved on.

Cousin Horace let himself down carefully into the low lawn chair. "I could almost believe I'd been here before, in some other life."

"Well, I keep telling you—you probably have." Pip laughed. He sat cross-legged on the stone wall above them, silhouetted against the starlit sky.

"You two, really—it's just the garden," said Gee from her chair. She laid her hand on Emma's head, which rested against her knee.

Then merriment rose again in Pip. "You may have been here before, Cousin Horace, but you better make sure you're here again, over Labor Day. It's Emma's sixteenth birthday and that's going to be one honey of a soiree, n'est-ce pas, Gee?"

"You'd better believe it, Pipper; I promised Emma a real send-off."

Then the moon appeared and began her rise, and they fell silent. The huge, nearly perfect sphere seemed to draw them with her as she mounted slowly into the sky. Paling the stars around her, she cast over the valley and Mount Ascutney, over Bell Brook Farm and the magical garden, a mysterious and opalescent glow. On and on they sat, mute, transfixed, without moving at all.

At last Gee broke the long silence. In a low husky voice she said:

"Ah, Moon of my Delight who know'st no wane,
The Moon of Heav'n is rising once again.
    How oft thereafter rising shall she look
Through this same Garden—"

Gee's voice ceased abruptly.

But Cousin Horace knew the end of the verse and spontaneously spoke the words, ". . . and after me—in vain!" Then, with infinite tenderness, he laid his veined old hand over Gee's; and Emma, ignorant of the poem, saw him.

He knows, Emma thought. Cousin Horace has guessed that Gee is sick. Has Pip?

But Pip, now lying spread-eagled on his back, as though in offering to the moon, merely said, "Twice, that's how oft. Two more full moons before Emma's birthday."

"You sure?" Emma asked, meaning the moon, but for some reason feeling a little stab of anxiety. She turned to look at her grandmother, and Gee leaned forward and said, in a low voice, for her ears alone, "I'm sure, pumpkin, that I can promise. I will be there for your birthday."

Pip, catching the words not meant for him, raised his head and turned it toward them. In the bright white moonlight Emma met her brother's eyes and saw the knowledge, dropped like a seed, take root and ripen.

"Okay, so what's going on, Emma?" Pip sat down on Emma's bed and regarded her sternly in the lamplight.

Emma continued to brush her hair.

"I have eyes, Emma. I can see she's thinner. She moves different, too. But otherwise she looks—or rather, seems—just like her old self, so what's up?"

"Having the family around over the weekend—it's the first time this summer there's been anything like a crowd. She likes it, but it makes her tired, that's all."

"Emma."

Emma stopped brushing her hair. In the mirror over the chest of drawers she caught Pip's eye.

"What is up?" he asked again.

Emma put down the brush. What was the use of lying to Pip? He knew her too well, he knew Gee too well.

"She's sick, isn't she?"

"Yes."

"Bad?"

"Probably."

"How 'probably'?"

"Well, she's going to have some kind of tests this week," Emma said bleakly. "They'll tell a lot more for sure."

"You're telling me she may die?"

The terror flew like a flock of birds through Emma, piercing her heart all over.

"Yes," she whispered.

"God," Pip said and turned to stare moodily at the moon-whitened hill outside Emma's north window.

Emma went into the bathroom and came back in her nightgown, and Pip moved to the end of the bed to make room for her to climb in.

Lying on her back, hoping for a little breeze, Emma looked up at the shepherdess.

"How do you feel?" Pip asked her after a while.

"Scared."

"Of what exactly?"

"Of dying. Of Gee dying. Of me dying."

"Well," said Pip. "Try not to be. Try to believe me."

"Five years ago, when you nearly died—"

"Or did...."

"Well, that time—"

"It was like . . . it was . . . it was very, very . . ." his voice trailed off. "All right," he said.

"For you."

"For me."

"How do you know it's the same for everyone?"

"Emma, you only know what you know."

"Meaning?"

"Meaning just that. I only know what I know. I can't make it be so for you."

Emma swallowed. "I almost understand," she said.

Gently Pip punched the summer blanket over her thigh. Then he wiped his hand across his eyes, and the two of them remained silent for a few minutes.

"I won't say a word, to anyone. But write me," Pip said, standing up. Suddenly he ducked down and kissed Emma's forehead. "Good night, Em."

"Goodnight, Pip," she said, startled and touched and reassured. Pip had never ever kissed her before.

Two days later, having obeyed Dr. Langdon's orders to take nothing at all for breakfast, Gee went to the new hospital in Winslow to have her tests.

"He said I'd be back by lunchtime, pumpkin," she said, brushing Emma's cheek with her finger-tips.

She is as frightened as I, thought Emma. How white she looks.

"Please, Gee, let me come with you. Even though I can't drive, it might make you feel better to have someone with you on the way back, if you're weak or something." Emma could hear her voice quaver.

Standing by the car, Gee folded her in her arms. "I'd much rather you stayed, darling; I'd feel better about leaving Chloe and the foal, for one thing; and anyway these are only X-rays. As a matter of fact, Jim Fothergill has insisted on following me back out here in his pickup, so you needn't worry." Buried in the hug, Emma was physically aware of Gee's distress. "Truly," Gee added. "And remember, Bertha will be here this morning." She kissed the top of Emma's head, got into the car, and drove off.

Emma did the only thing she knew to do: She went to the barn. Over the Fourth of July weekend she had neglected some of the details of her chores. The brief invasion of family and the advent of the colt had broken the rhythm of her otherwise unswerving routine, and for the two days since Pip and Cousin Horace left, she and Gee had been caught up in setting the house to rights again, stripping the beds and collecting bits and pieces of toys from unexpected corners. (Emma had found the fierce plastic head of Darth Vader in the butter dish and forty-three pieces of the Lego set scattered far and wide, from the toe of one of her sneakers to Gee's tooth mug.)

Meanwhile she had her own work to do in the barn, and she threw herself into it in hopes of dispelling the anxiety that gripped and at times almost paralyzed her. Try as she might, however, Emma was unable wholly to pay attention to her work. Only when it came time to deal with Chloe and the foal did her fear relax its sharp hold.

Chloe had a small pasture to herself, off the foaling quarters, and since the day after her accouchement she and Yankee Doodle spent most of their time outdoors. The colt was undeniably beautiful, more beautiful, even, than Chloe's first, whose long-legged image had briefly adorned Gee's bathroom.

A light bay, his black, beaverlike tail and spiky black mane setting off the reddish-brown coat, Yankee had, above all, "a nice eye," as Gee said. A nice eye in a royal head, Emma added to herself.

"You're just perfect, that's all, just plain perfect," and she approached him slowly, with a foal halter dangling casually from one hand. "And the time has come for you to get used to this."

She held out the flimsy leather contraption. The foal backed off, already surprisingly sure of foot, and Chloe raised her head from the grass to inspect what Emma carried and watch her closely. Step by step, willing the foal to hold still, Emma reached him and scratched his neck with her free hand.

"Oh, so booooooful," she cooed.

Still wary, his long furry ears pricked toward her, Yankee snorted through his little velvet nose. Just as Emma was about to slide her arm around his neck and slip the halter over his head, the foal decided that the end of the world had come. He whirled around to the other side of his mother, staggering slightly on his long spindly legs. Eyes wide, he peered at Emma from the safety of Chloe's flanks. Chloe returned to grazing.

So Emma, amused, and engaged by the contest, began all over again. Once the gander drove her helter-skelter over the gate, but she ventured back. Eventually she cornered Yankee between Chloe and the fence and managed to put the halter on. Squatting with her back against the shed, she watched him shake his head and dance drunkenly around the paddock before butting his nose up under Chloe's belly for a snack; then, grudgingly used to Emma's presence, he let himself down limb by limb into the patch of shade cast by his mother. Quickly Emma slipped off the halter, and the foal fell fast asleep.

Now what? her mind cried in alarm.

Like a stone dropping in a pond, fear rippled through her chest and lapped at her heart. Emma looked at her watch and was surprised to see that it was nearly noon. Bertha Simmons would have left, and Emma had not even said hello to her. Now the house would be empty.

I must think of something else to do, she thought and jumped to her feet.

At that moment the sound of Gee's car reached her ears; and as she hurried up to the lawn, torn between apprehension and relief, Jim's blue pick-up crested the rise.

"Thanks, Jim," Gee was saying briskly as she stepped out of the car. She patted the top of Emma's head on her way to the house. On the step she stopped and looked back.

She looks so normal, thought Emma. It must be okay.

"And Jim," said Gee. "It really was a great moral support, having you escort me home. Though quite unnecessary," she added with a touch of tartness and smiled. "I'm sorry you won't stay for lunch."

The screen door slammed behind her.

"Hello, Emma," said Jim.

"How do you think she is?" Emma asked him, not daring to take comfort in Gee's spry manner.

"She seemed very composed, very—well—chipper, even, when I met her in the hospital parking lot. I don't know what to think."

"When will Dr. Langdon have anything to tell us?"

"I don't know. I guess later today."

"Oh, God," said Emma.

"I know what you mean, Em, but in a way it will be better to have it all over with."

Emma gave a little shiver in the hot July day. "Stay, Jim, have lunch with us, please do. It'll help, having you around."

A fleeting expression, which she did not try to interpret, crossed his face. He ran a hand through his thick unruly hair, trying to bring it to order.

"Yes. Of course. Yes, I'd love to," he said. "If you think Gee means it," and he smiled shyly at her.

They had a gay picnic lunch, the three of them, sitting out under the tree-house maple. Kind Bertha had surprised them with her famous cold vegetable puree. Even Gee ate it. She regaled them with a drama she had witnessed in the hospital parking lot on her way in to be tested. A toddler had balked at going to the doctor. Escaping from his mother, he had crawled under a two-seater car and would not budge. When Gee left the scene the young mother, attempting to disguise her frustration with a saccharine voice, was kneeling on the asphalt paving with her head under the car.

"Come out, Fred," she was pleading. "Come out now and Momma will give you a nice big bag of M & M's."

When they finished eating, a silence fell upon them, filled with the rustle of the maple leaves above as an afternoon breeze caressed the farm. Emma felt sunlight mottle her skin in shifting patterns as the shade stirred.

At last Jim cleared his throat. "I really ought to be getting back to the office—" He glanced questioningly at Emma.

"Of course you must," said Gee. "I'll get the papers you left here last time."

But she made no move to rise.

"I have to tell you something," Gee said. "Those tests . . . I failed them . . . and Dr. Langdon has agreed to stop treatment."

Jim bowed his head and stared at the lawn. For a moment Emma felt as though she had slipped out of her body and hung suspended in the leaves of the maple tree; then the terrible thump of her heart in the silence brought her back to her senses.

Gee spoke. "I'm so sorry, darling Emma, to have to tell you this." She turned to Jim. "And you, too, my friend. And I am going to ask something very difficult of you both. You see, although I do not have very long, I wish to *live* what time is left me. I am not afraid anymore, not now, anyway. I feel no pain.

"If it does not place too great a burden on you, my Emma, I want to keep this to ourselves as long as possible."

She leaned forward and took Emma's hand. "*Is* this too much? I have thought about it a great deal, because I more than half-expected these results, and I realize that in many ways it is selfish of me. You are free, in good conscience, my Emma, to go home—no, no," as Emma gave a little cry of protest, "I only wanted to give you the choice."

Gee squeezed Emma's hand and looked away until she regained full control of her voice. "I'm glad you want to stay, darling." Then, in her usual voice, she said, "But if we tell the others, nothing will ever be the same again. They will treat me differently; they will want to come to help, because they will think I am an invalid. Can you manage this, Em, this knowing?"

"Yes," said Emma, and she felt curiously calm and unafraid; only a queer heaviness seemed to enter her chest, expelling the anxiety, now that the suspense was over. "I can manage, Gee. Will it— will you—will we have the whole summer?"

"Oh, yes, pumpkin, I'm sure we will." Gee let go of Emma's hand and, as though in blessing, gestured at the house, the lawn, the sky above. "And what a summer it is. I don't believe there has ever been such a perfect summer," she said.

So it continued, day after day of beautiful weather, neither too hot nor too dry. Little showers fell at night—enough to water Gee's gardens, but not too much to spoil the new hay crop, which John cut in patches. The vegetables ripened and pro-liferated, the delphiniums bloomed early and grew enormous, so that Mrs. Brown, Gee's roommate from college days, remarked, when she and her husband came to visit, "I declare, Georgia, from a distance they look like little blue pine trees!"

With surprising ease Emma resumed her normal routine. She was glad the Browns had come. They were just the right people to practice on, she decided, rather taken aback to discover how easily deception came to her, how easily she pretended that all was well at Bell Brook Farm. When Emma tried to analyze why this was so after the Browns left, she realized it was because it was true: For now, all *was* well at Bell Brook Farm. Only the strange heaviness—the heaviness of dread —would not go away.

I'll get used to it in time, she guessed.

For several days they had no visitors, not even Jim. On the tenth of July his firm called him to New York on business. Before leaving, he told them it sounded like a challenging case. "Otherwise, they'd have a hard time prying me from Vermont."

Instinctively Gee and Emma resumed the pace of their first weeks together. Gee's illness was never mentioned, nor did it affect the tenor of their life. They simply took each day as it came and relished it.

On July fourteenth Emma got a letter from Mary Jo. Even the envelope smelled of fish, and the pages inside reeked where Mary Jo's hand had rested on them. Emma read avidly but with mixed feelings about Mary Jo's summer—the daily grind at the cannery; the other workers, many of them her own age; the parties on weekends off, with her boyfriend—Emma whistled on reading what the two of them had been up to—the poor pay; the new landscape; the smell that went everywhere with Mary Jo, "but you get used to it and Charlie doesn't seem to mind." I should say not, thought

Emma, from the sound of it. All in all Mary Jo sure is having a different summer from me.

Emma put the letter down and gazed out her window to the barnyard. It was a day out of a poem: balmy, languorous, filled with light; in the garden she could hear the snip, snip, snip of Gee's clippers.

"But I still wouldn't change places with her," she said out loud. "Why, I wonder?"

Emma even found she was able to leave Gee alone for periods of time without worrying. I'll save that for when the summer is over, she told herself. After the party, when I go. . . . Quickly a door closed in her mind, and she hastened to the barn to saddle Hal.

One evening Joey Perry, having just received his driver's license, called Emma and invited her to go to the movies with him, and Emma accepted.

When she told her grandmother, Gee was delighted. "Oh, *good*," she said. "I've been worried about you seeing people your own age."

"You needn't, Gee."

Emma enjoyed her evening with Joey. After the movie they went to Dino's for pizza.

"What do you *do* all day, Emma? God, here it is the middle of July, and I've only seen you once."

Emma explained her summer project. She knew enough not to tell him in detail, having seen Pip's eyes glaze over when she described her barn work. Joey did not seem the least bit bored, however; in fact Joey asked her to tell him more.

"No, now it's your turn," Emma said. "I heard you telling Pip you liked working for Ray Flanagan. Doesn't your head split from all the noise?"

Ray Flanagan was a logger.

"You get used to it. Want to come watch some day? I'll give you earphones. You can listen to music while we work. It's kind of neat to see those big machines in action."

"I know. I remember Pip and I watched one time and nearly got killed by the 'dozer."

"What! You're kidding! How come I didn't know that? Come on, Emma, tell."

Emma was flattered by Joey's interest. It *was* nice being with someone so nearly her age—Joey was sixteen-and-a-half—and she was about to ask him if he wanted to come for supper the following evening, when something about the way he was gazing at her made her hold her tongue.

It was suddenly clear to her that Joey was no longer just the kid from the next valley over, a childish summer companion to her and Pip ever since she could remember, but Joey with a car and a license and a man's job. Better to think over a bit whether she wanted to encourage this new Joey.

"Want to go to the movies next week?" he was asking.

"Joey, it depends who's coming up," Emma hedged, and was relieved to see Lettie Reynolds approaching their booth; her boyfriend was with her.

"Hi, Emma," said Lettie, nodding to Joey. "I'm sorry I didn't call you—I've been meaning to. How about tomorrow? Will you ride with me tomorrow?"

"I'd *love* to," said Emma, adding quickly, for Joey's benefit; "There's no one staying with us now, so I can go for a long ride, if you can too, Lettie."

"Done," said Lettie. "Let's meet at White Rock at two and take it from there."

When Lettie moved off, with her hand in her boyfriend's arm, Emma said, "We'd better go, Joey. I've had an awfully nice time—of course I'd like to go to the movies with you again."

And it was true. Emma had enjoyed her evening out very much.

Lettie and Emma met on the dot of two o'clock the next day, Lettie riding up White Rock hill from the west, Emma from the east. After a preliminary mock skirmish to establish who was boss, the two horses apparently agreed to a draw and got along well together. Lettie's thoroughbred was young and unfinished, very like Hal only a few years ago, and Emma was pleased to see how far Gee's big chestnut had come.

They rode for miles, crossing one range of hills after another on trails and old logging roads, letting the horses gallop along the tracks that were flat enough, bushwhacking occasionally when they lost their way. Often they walked or jogged abreast, chatting companionably about their horses, the people they knew in common, Lettie and her boyfriend.

"Are you going to marry him, then?" Emma asked with the awe that she always felt at the thought of any friend of hers actually getting married.

"I guess so. Later. When we can own our own house."

Emma longed to ask what it was like to be really in love, but Lettie didn't *look* especially in love, or different in any way at all. Emma assumed you were bound to look different when in love. Hadn't her aunts? She cast back in her mind, but the last aunt had married five years ago and Emma could not remember exactly how she had looked.

Lettie smiled at her. "Are you thinking of falling in love?"

Emma blushed. How on earth had Lettie read her thoughts? "Who with?" she returned.

"Well, what about that guy you were with the other night—Joey Perry? He's a good kid from what I hear, and he sure is stuck on you."

"Oh, Lettie! For heaven's sake, Pip and I have been playing with Joey since we were little."

"Little people grow up, Emma. That's what it's all about."

"You act as though I could just decide to fall in love—with Joey or anyone else."

"Not exactly 'decide'; 'allow' yourself, maybe. Hey, here's the fork. Look, I've got to get home. I'm waitressing tonight at the tavern. This has been great. Let's do it again, OK?"

"*OK*," said Emma, and with a farewell wave she squeezed her legs against Hal's sides and sent him homeward up the long hill.

The next day Emma came out of the barnyard just as Gee was walking from the garden to the house with a basket of cut flowers over one arm.

Something's different. The thought came to her before Emma could stop it.

She watched Gee slowly mount the stone steps into the Music Room, pause halfway, as though to catch her breath, and almost pull herself through the doorway.

Yet when Emma joined her in the kitchen moments later, prepared to ask her if she felt all right, Gee greeted her cheerfully from her stool at the table where she perched, cutting stems; so Emma said nothing. But the weight in her chest, which she had been able, one way or another—her work, Gee's outward well-being—to come to terms with, stirred heavily, and from that moment on, guardedly, Emma watched her grandmother with an even sharper eye.

Jim's little blue pickup appeared outside the kitchen one morning, just as Emma was finishing her breakfast. Gee sat by the window reading yesterday's newspaper. When she saw who had come, a smile lit her face, so transforming it that Emma was struck by the contrast with how frail her grandmother had come to look in repose.

"My dear Jim, back from New York," said Gee, as the lawyer came through the door. Emma noticed that she did not rise. "We've missed you."

Gee laid down her paper and held out both hands to him.

"Hi, Jim, how's the big city?" asked Emma, and she realized how glad she was that he was back. The heaviness even seemed to lighten at the thought that now there would be two of them again.

"Big, Em, and dirty, but I love it anyway. The firm wants me to take on some clients in Africa." He kissed Gee's cheek. "It's great to be home, though."

"Come down and see how the foal has grown before you go, will you?" Emma asked as the phone began to ring. She went into the hall to answer it and reappeared a minute later to say to her grandmother, "Gee, that's Joey. He wants to know if I'll go to the movies with him tonight. What do you think?" I'm beginning not to want to leave you alone, Emma realized with a little chill.

"What do I think?" Gee laughed. "I think you should go, little goose."

When Emma returned from talking to Joey, Jim and Gee were bending over an official-looking document. Jim looked up as Emma passed through the kitchen.

"See you in the barn," he said.

"That was her will, wasn't it?" Emma asked the moment Jim appeared in the barn doorway.

"Yep."

"How do you think she looks?"

"Not well. She's gone downhill some, just since I've been away."

"Yes. I only really noticed it the other day."

"That's because you see her all the time. And you can't get away from it, being the only one in the family to know."

Emma felt a little stab of guilt. She forced herself to look straight at Jim.

"I told Pip," she said. "He—he'd just about guessed, the night before he and Cousin Horace left; but Jim, truly, if Pip had been living here this summer as usual, Gee would have."

"Emma. Emma. Dear Emma." Jim took her hands in his. "It's all right about Pip. You know it is." He looked down at their clasped hands and let Emma's go.

"Yes, I do know. You see we are very close, we three. . . . But listen, Jim, if she's really getting worse, do you think we can just go on and on not saying anything to Mom and Dan and the aunts? I mean, she talks to them on the phone, and they're all planning to come up at one time or another, later on in the summer and they don't know a *thing*—even Pam and Libba, not really. It's all going to come as an awful shock, just seeing her— I'd be mad if I were them."

"Oh, God, Em, it must be so damned hard for you." Jim leaned back against a stall door with his hands in his pockets. "But if we just keep telling ourselves: Gee comes first; this is the way she wants to do it—would that help you? Make everything else sort of fall into place?"

"Yes . . . it does . . . and she's not *that* bad." It made her feel better just saying it. "She just *looks* worse, she *acts* pretty well, really. Boy, is she ever getting crafty about visitors, though; somehow or other she's managed to put everyone off for the time being." Emma picked up her broom. "Oh, God," she said, beginning to sweep.

"Come. Show me Yankee," said Jim. He started to hold out his hand, then put it back in his pocket.

Emma led him down the aisle to Chloe's quarters, stalwartly fending off the gander, and was pleased by Jim's evident surprise at the growth of the colt.

"Here, hold the gate open for me, will you? I'm going to put them in the orchard pasture—they need more room and more grass now."

Emma took Chloe by the halter and, with Yankee gamboling behind, led her to the bigger field. Jim closed the gate and came to stand next to her in the sun, and together they watched the beautiful outlandish colt cavorting around the pasture as though mad.

"Have you been able to keep a coherent account of the barn work for your project?" Jim asked. "What with everything else on your mind, it must take quite an effort."

"Oh, good grief, yes. I've got this project down in so much detail, it'll take the judges a week just to read it. I guess I'll have to do some editing. It's been a godsend, though, having to pay attention."

Jim looked at her. His hazel eyes were so full of kindness that Emma was touched. "I bet it has," he said and appeared to be going to say something more. When he did not, Emma looked away, at Chloe and the colt, at the pond beyond the orchard, at Ascutney rising over the wooded hills to the south.

"It's so beautiful here," she said sadly. "And it will never be the same again."

She felt Jim's hand on her shoulder and turned to him.

"Listen to me, Emma," he said, gripping her shoulder with his long fingers. "It will always be beautiful. Always. Somehow we'll manage to keep the farm in the family, even if it has to be rented or left empty for a few years. Nothing is the same forever, but this place will always be beautiful." He removed his hand and looked at it, then pushed his wrist forward to see his watch. "Golly," he said. "Look at the time. I'm supposed to turn in a brief before noon. So long, Em."

Lightly he tapped her shoulder and strode off through the barnyard.

"What did you think of it?" asked Joey, as he and Emma emerged from the movie house in Winslow.

"I liked it okay—it was pretty funny in places, but I'm beginning to agree with Gee—all that violence, it bends your mind out of shape."

"Oh, come on, Em, it was meant to be funny. You laughed yourself; I saw you."

"I know, I know, but I didn't really *like* laughing."

"I liked the part where the car drives off the cliff and the guy—"

"That's just what I mean—oh, well, never mind. It was fun going, anyway, Joey. Next time you have to let *me* treat *you*."

"We'll see about that," said Joey importantly, and he took her arm. "How about a pizza now?"

"Joey, you know Gee was sick today—some kind of upset stomach. I think I ought to get home."

Joey's face fell. For a moment Emma was afraid he was going to sulk, but he only said, in his usual good-natured way, "Okay, if you insist. Next time, though, let's have a real date."

On the way out to Bell Brook Farm Joey drove slowly.

"You're going to be a junior next year, aren't you?" he asked.

"Yup. And *you're* going to be a senior. And Pip graduated this year! God, Joey, just think how grown-up we're all getting."

"What do you plan to do after school? College?"

"I hope so. You?"

"I'd like to try the University of Vermont. My grades are pretty good, so I guess they'll take me, but I dunno, Em, I'm not sure college is the place for me. I like the outdoors too much, and most of all, I want to see the world before I get too old to. You want to see the world?"

"Well, yes, someday I guess I'd like to see the world. What do your parents think?"

"They prettty much leave it up to me. I know they're hoping I'll like the university, but they're trying not to let it show."

Emma gave a little laugh. "Parents," she said affectionately. "They try so hard."

At the foot of Gee's lane, Joey drew up to the side of the road and cut the engine.

"Just for a bit. Let's sit here just for a bit and talk," he said, flicking off the headlights.

Uh-oh, thought Emma. Not now. Not Joey.

"You got a boyfriend back home?" asked Joey.

"Nope."

"I don't have a girlfriend, either. Last year I was kind of hung up on Polly Langdon—you know, Doc Langdon's daughter—but, I dunno, it just sort of came apart in Christmas vacation. She went to New York with her family and I went skiing in Canada with some of the guys and when school started again, it was just plain old *over*."

"I know, that's happened to a lot of my friends. Some of them, though, they've been going steady for more than a year."

"That's what I'd like to do," said Joey. He slid his arm along the back of the car seat and let his fingers dangle over Emma's right shoulder.

Uh-oh, thought Emma again.

"Boy, you sure have changed," said Joey in a husky voice.

"How do you mean?" Emma could feel herself stiffening.

"You're—I don't know—you're older, and well, you always were pretty, Em, but now—"

Suddenly Joey leaned forward and kissed Emma on the mouth. His lips were soft, his breath clean, his touch, as he drew her to him with his right arm and laid his left hand on her neck, gentle and undemanding.

Now just try, thought Emma rapidly. *Allow* yourself to think Joey is your prince come true.

Joey raised his head. "Em?" he said.

"Yes," Emma whispered.

Joey kissed her again.

It *is* pleasant, Emma decided this time. Her body felt warm and as though it were waking up out of a delicious sleep. I like Joey a whole lot better than the boys back home who want to do this.

She put her right hand on his neck, then slid it around so that they hugged each other.

This is *nice*, she thought.

Then Joey began to kiss her a little more forcefully and one hand slipped down her arm and onto her breast. Emma pulled back, and immediately Joey let her go. They were both breathing quite fast.

After a little while Joey took her hand in his and said, "Will you be my girl, Emma?"

"Let me think about it, Joey," she answered. "You were almost like a brother before. I'd have to get used to the idea. I don't even know if I *want* to have a boyfriend." She opened the door of the car. "I want to go home, now," she said. "And I want to walk up."

Then, turning to him and seeing his shadowed face, she touched her lips with two fingers and laid them on his cheek.

"Good night, Joey," she said.

"Good night, Emma. I'll call you."

Walking up the lane after Joey drove off, Emma reviewed the scene in his car. The memory of Joey's lips on hers brought back a warm sensation in her loins, her belly, the backs of her knees, even her toes. She felt stirred as she had not since the time, three years ago, when that friend of Pip's had forced her to a kind of fever by his fumbling, fierce embraces; but then he had gone too far and made Emma feel tainted and ashamed.

This evening she had decided, yes *decided*, she said to Lettie in her mind, to let Joey kiss her and to kiss him back, and she had allowed herself to enjoy it. She liked the feel of Joey well enough, and she was fond of him, but did she really want to commit herself to being his girlfriend? The further she progressed along the lane, the less potent was the memory of his caresses.

Well, I don't have to decide anything tonight, she said aloud, and stopped to listen to the frogs in the pond. All around her fireflies blinked on and off. The night air was warm, even sultry, the sky less brilliant than it had been for so long, the stars muted by a thin haze.

The weather's changing, she thought as she crested the rise.

Long panels of light lay across the lawn from

the Music Room windows. Emma started for the door, her feet soundless on the grass. Reaching for the knob, she looked into the room and froze.

There, in her favorite chair, her head bowed and one hand cupped across her eyes, sat Gee. She was weeping. Emma could see the tears sliding down the contorted face, the thin shoulders curved as though to ward off prying eyes.

Whirling back from the light, Emma flattened herself against the side of the house. Her mouth was so dry she could not swallow, and a pulse fluttered in her throat.

I must go to her, she thought, terrified. But she doesn't want you to know, another part of her spoke.

What to do? Emma had never seen her grandmother cry; she could not bear it. Cautiously, she edged up to the window, thinking to duck past it and approach the house again, whistling loudly.

When she glanced in, however, Gee was sitting upright, both hands in her lap, her face white but composed. Emma opened the door.

"Why, hello, darling," said Gee in a perfectly normal voice. "How come I didn't hear Joey's car?"

"I walked up the lane just to stretch my legs," Emma answered, trying not to look at Gee's face, which still bore the trace of tears, she saw now. In her chest the ever-present dread stirred sluggishly.

"How was the movie?"

"You would have hated it, Gee. Lots of people got killed and it was very noisy."

"Let's listen to Fred Astaire's sailors before we go to bed," said Gee.

So Emma put on the cassette and they sat together in the lamplight, and each in her own way was soothed and uplifted by the jaunty little song.

The next morning Emma woke up just before dawn, stifled by a sense of oppression. The sheet stuck to her damply, the air felt heavy to breathe, and, without raising her head to look out the window, Emma knew the weather had indeed changed.

She knew, too, that the real heaviness lay inside her, engendered by anxiety. A new and heavy kind of anxiety had invaded her while she slept; like an unbidden shadow it clung to her inside and out, turning her limbs to lead and causing a physical ache in her chest.

Nervously, taking refuge in bodily action, she sat up. Her dear little room looked gray and forlorn in the sunless predawn light. Outside, the sky was hazy.

If she got up now, Emma knew, even before her grandmother, Dumbo would hear and wag his tail, thumping it on the hall floor outside Gee's room and waking her. But she could not—no, she could not—stay in bed.

Emma jumped up. Panic fluttered in her stomach, the backs of her knees felt wobbly, the palms of her hands damp and slick, as she pulled on her clothes.

Soon she is going to die.

Like her observation of Gee's slackened step the other day, the perception appeared—whole, relentless—in Emma's mind. Up to now, when she could bring herself to confront her grandmother's circumstances at all, she said to herself: Gee is going to live while I am here; she promised. She promised to be here for my birthday.

Now doubt, like the anxiety that had stolen upon her during the night, infiltrated her, and she did not know how to handle it.

Holding her sneakers in one hand, she pulled the handle of her door toward her and pressed down on the thumb latch. Soundlessly the bar on the other side rose; Emma nudged the door open and peeked into the hall. Immediately Dumbo lifted his head and smiled at her, raising his long heavy tail high and whacking it down on the hardwood floor.

Emma glared at him. "Sh-h-h!" she hissed as loud as she dared.

Obediently, Dumbo stopped his tail in midflight, let it fall back on to his cushion, and, with a sleepy groan, resettled his nose between Witch's paws.

Emma tiptoed down the stairs, avoiding the

squeaky ones, which she knew by heart, and let herself out the front door.

Down in the barn the cement floor was wet, and chaff stuck to Emma's arms. The humidity caused her to move slowly through her morning chores, but by the time she had finished, the familiar routine had gone a long way to restoring her equanimity.

When she came out of the barn, she saw that clouds had collected on the western horizon and were moving raggedly across the hazy sky.

"It's partly the weather," she said to herself as her gut twisted uneasily. "And hunger. That's it, I'm hungry now."

But when she went into the kitchen and greeted her grandmother, Emma found that she was not hungry after all. They sat for a while listening to the weather report, which warned of thunderstorms, and then parted, Gee to her desk and Emma to her room to work on her journal.

During the morning Gee staked the remaining delphiniums and tied tarpaulins over the cushioned chairs under the tree-house maple. When Emma came down for lunch, she found her grandmother sitting at the kitchen table, tipping a pile of beans.

"I thought I'd better pick them all before it rains," she said.

"Whew, it's hot, and *heavy*." Emma, at the sink,

ran cold water over her arms and hands and cupped it onto her face. "I don't even have the energy to swim."

"Have some iced tea," said Gee.

Emma dried herself off and looked out the window.

"Good grief, the sky is getting black," she said. "After lunch I think I'll put everyone except Chloe and Yankee in the barnyard. The sheep, too. That way they'll all be able to get under the shed when it rains, and Chloe and the colt can just stay where they are. I'm glad I didn't put them out this morning."

Gee set an egg-salad sandwich on the table and watched Emma eat half of it.

"Oh, I forgot to tell you—Joey called. I told him you'd call him back."

"Okay, I will, later. Do you want me to do anything in the garden when I come up? I won't be long down there." Emma stood up and on a sudden impulse leaned over her grandmother and kissed her on the cheek. "You would tell me, wouldn't you, Gee, if there was anything I could do?"

Gee smiled up at her. "*Were.* 'If there *were* anything you could do,' because there isn't, pumpkin. It's all done, thank you just the same."

At last the storm broke. Rain fell suddenly in sheets and jagged lightning split the sky, turning their world an eerie sickly green. Simultaneously wave after wave of thunder cracked overhead, paused, cracked again, and with a terrible roar broke over the farm, shaking the house before clattering away down the valley.

The wind, which all afternoon had sprung up and fallen back in aimless hot gusts, without origin or aim, now became a concentrated force, whirling relentlessly through the huge maples, driving the rain sideways, so that Emma, flying around the corner of the house to secure the unlatched and wildly banging cellar door, felt as though her eyebrows might be stripped away in the horizontal cascades of water that assaulted her.

When she bolted back to safety, the wind tore the door out of her hand and slammed it shut behind her. Drenched, Emma pulled off her sweatshirt. She watched her grandmother filling kettles.

"The electricity's bound to go any moment," Gee said, moving slowly but purposefully through the kitchen. "And then we'll have no pump for the water. Our bathtub is full, too."

Beneath the clamor of the ran and thunder they heard a sharp little ping.

"That'll be the phone," they said together, and smiled.

"Jinx," said Emma, drying herself as well as she could on a beach towel. Although more than a little frightened by the violence of the storm, she was beginning to enjoy it, too. Here was something concrete, real, and visible to deal with.

The kitchen had become as dark as evening, and

Emma reached for the string over the table to turn on the light. In vain.

"It's gone," she said unnecessarily.

"Imagine, only four o'clock, and here we sit. ..."

A loud crack sounded over the wing of the house, followed at once by a crash and—above the tumult of the storm—the noise of breaking glass. Looking toward the Music Room, Emma saw the pictures on the wall jiggle and hang askew.

"Oh, Lord," said Gee. In the lightning flashes her face was white and deeply shadowed. "It's a branch down, onto the roof. Big one, too, it sounds. Run see if there's a leak, Em. Here"—opening the door to the cellar stairs and fumbling along a shelf—"here's the flashlight." She turned it on and handed it to Emma. "I'll get the kerosene for the lamps."

Upstairs, in the room over the Music Room, Emma could hear the limb from the maple scraping the roof, caught, no doubt, on the chimney. One pane was out and another was about to go as the lesser branches flapped and flattened against the window. Rain blew in through the opening and in the pale wavering light of her flashlight, Emma saw wet leaves littering the rug. Rivulets of water ran along the baseboard and under the desk.

Quickly, her heart racing a little at this new proof of the storm's power, she stuffed a small pillow into the opening; then she took the beach towel from around her shoulders and pressed it on the rug with her foot to mop up the worst of the rain, running back and forth to the bathroom to squeeze it out.

Absorbed in her task, she only gradually became aware of a general lightening of both the sound and visibility in the room. The storm no longer seemed to be directly overhead; the wind had diminished; there were longer pauses between the flashes of lightning and rolls of thunder; and, she noticed, as she swept up the leaves and broken glass, the beam of the flashlight had almost disappeared as daylight reemerged.

When she looked out the window she was astonished to see that, across Bell Brook valley, pale sunlight washed the hills. Before her eyes it spread, as the turbulent black clouds moved eastward, and within moments the soaked lawn and restless maples glittered wetly under a blue summer sky. The storm was over.

Carrying the debris, Emma ran down the stairs of the wing, through the Music Room and into the kitchen.

"Gee, isn't it—"

But there was no sign of her grandmother.

"Gee!" Emma called again.

A faint sound reached her ears; she could not identify it, but the hair on her arms stood on end in alarm.

"*Gee.* Where are you?"

Again the sound. This time Emma heard it more

clearly; it was a human voice, halfway between a moan and a sigh, and it came from the cellar.

Emma looked at the door to the cellar stairway. It hung open. She rushed to the head of the stairs and looked down and saw Gee lying crumpled at the foot.

Emma was sure her heart had stopped for good, so long did her moment of horror last.

"Gee," she breathed.

Below her, Gee stirred, raised her head, and said, "This is unbelievably foolish of me, but I missed my footing when I reached for the kerosene."

"Oh, Gee." Emma started down the dark stairway.

By the time she got to the bottom, Gee was half-sitting, leaning on one forearm. Emma, her breath high and cold in her throat, knelt beside her.

"Gee," she whimpered again.

"Believe it or not, pumpkin, I think I'm OK. Maybe a rib or two cracked. Very shook up."

Gee panted lightly. Her face looked to Emma's frightened eyes like a skull, so dark were the eye sockets; the skin over her grandmother's forehead glistened damply in the gloomy unlit cellar.

"Very shook up," Gee repeated. "And quite bruised," she added in a brisker tone, shifting her weight to the other elbow and raising herself to a sitting position. "Now let's see if I can stand." She held out her hand to Emma.

"Oh, Gee, do you think you should even try, yet?"

"Yup. Pull."

The strength of Gee's grip both surprised and reassured Emma. Together, slowly, they raised her to her feet. Leaning against the wall, Gee closed her eyes.

"Don't think I . . . can get . . . upstairs." Her breathing was fast, the voice thin. "'Fraid you better get . . . Dr. Langdon."

"How?" Emma's voice quavered when she saw her grandmother begin to shake.

Gee slid slowly down the wall until she sat on the bottom step.

"I'm fine, like this," she said after a little while, in an almost normal voice. "I *think* I'm fine, period. But even if I *could* get up the stairs you'd better ask him to come. Something feels funny in my chest."

"Gee, how am I going to call him? There's no phone."

Gee didn't answer; all Emma heard was the shallow, quickened breath.

Then: "Take Hal," Gee said. "Ride to the Lunts'—only a mile-and-a-half." She paused. "John can drive to the hospital or a phone that works—whatever. . . . Go along, Em." She fell silent.

Emma kissed her and sped up the stairs, amazed

that she could make her body obey her, considering the weight it carried near her heart. At the top she flicked the light switch up in case the electricity came on again. Already in jeans, she pulled on her boots and fled out the door into the shining wet afternoon.

No time for a saddle, Emma decided, when she caught Hal. Having to think, having to concentrate on Hal, all helped to settle her. She grasped his mane, swung up onto the tall back, and sent him into the puddled lane at a canter.

At first Hal spooked at the dripping foliage on either side. Unaccustomed to such a hasty departure, unused to being ridden bareback, and aware of Emma's tension, he trembled and snorted and swerved all the way to the end. Then something of his rider's authority seemed to come through to him, and he began to work with her.

Emma negotiated him around the hairpin turn, steered to one side of an enormous puddle, and urged him down the road as fast as she dared.

Almost five—John'll be finished milking. What if he's not there? What if Sonia isn't either? Their phone will be out—someone's *got* to be there, to drive Gee or go for help. Now, cool it, cool it, of *course* someone will be there. . . .

Rounding a curve, Emma saw a fallen birch across the road.

No time to stop, can't go around, OK, Hal—

she headed him for the left-hand bank where the hurdle was lowest—here we go.

Hal took off well before the tree, sailed high over it, and landed faultlessly on the further side. For an instant Emma feared he would slip in the slick mud and that they would both go down, but the big chestnut collected himself immediately and thundered on, with Emma clinging to him.

At the foot of the hill, instead of taking the main dirt road, Emma swung Hal onto the shortcut— an old track now flooded with rainwater but sound of footing, Emma knew, and relatively flat. Down the trail Hal splashed at a gallop, throwing showers of mud over them both. Where the track veered right, Emma turned him left; they jumped a ditch into John's long lower cornfield and headed for the barn, flying down the long, wet, rustling rows of corn.

Almost there—don't think about woodchuck holes—just let him go flat out—we'll make it, we'll make it, we'll make it. The prickly leaves of the cornstalks scratched her arms. What if they're not home? Stop that, they have to be . . . begin to slow down, now, down now, Hal, whoa, down now, Hal, whoa, whoa, whoa, Hal.

Bit by bit she brought the big horse in, collecting him back into her control. By the time they reached the cow yard near the barn, though Hal still pulled at the bit, Emma was able to bring him to a halt.

She swung off his back and almost fell when she hit the ground, so weak were her knees from the ride. Hal's sides heaved, and white froth flecked the sweat-dark, rain-dark hide.

Hastily, Emma tied the reins to a fence post. As she climbed the gate into the cow yard, she was instantly aware of its quiet. No sound of milking machines, no clank of shovels or pails, no voices. Only the low hum of the generator in the milk house, the stirring of the herd in their stanchions in the barn. Worse, there were no vehicles in the yard.

"John!" Emma called, knowing it was useless.

She ran to the house, hoping against hope that Sonia's car was around the corner and Sonia in the kitchen fixing supper. A note on the back porch caught her eye. She read it.

"Honey—Stove's out. Phone's out. I've gone to pick up a new blade in Winslow. Meet me at Dino's at 6. Treat you to supper. J."

Emma almost cried. A whine came from high in her throat, but she clenched her hands, digging her nails into the palms, until the sound ceased.

Winslow's too *far*, she wailed in her mind. Already a mile-and-a-half farther than Bell Brook Farm. How far are the telephone lines down? she wondered. If the storm blew from west to east, then maybe it missed South Woodbury. Certainly the lines of all their neighbors along Bell Brook would be down.

If we cut straight south through the woods, using trails and logging roads all the way, we'll enter South Woodbury from Morgan Hill—that's only about five, five and a half miles. In her head she plotted their course, cutting corners all the way. Pip would marvel, she thought to herself, surprised by her own cunning.

South Woodbury had no doctor, no store, no gas station; but it did have a collection of houses, and presumably all the houses had phones.

About halfway down Morgan Hill, Emma wiped the face of her watch against her knee and looked at it. Five twenty-five. The thought of Gee sitting alone in pain in the dark cellar for three-quarters of an hour or more made her groan, and she squeezed her legs against Hal's muddy flanks to urge him on.

Unquestionably he was tiring. The road was slippery and roughened by the cloudburst, littered with small branches and overturned stones. A couple of cars must have made it through since the storm, leaving unexpected hidden ruts in the mud.

Hal floundered his way down the steep hill, and Emma, exhausted, clung on as best she could.

I cannot bear this, Emma thought. I cannot bear any of this much longer; it's too much. I cannot bear it.

To her horror, she was furious at Gee; but to

Hal she cooed, "We can do it, we can do it, we can do it."

Still the village lay out of sight. Just as Emma felt herself giving way, letting panic sweep over her as it had in the tree house, there came to her ears the sound of a car approaching up the hill, and in a moment it hove into view. It was a small blue pickup.

Emma began to sob. Reining Hal to a stop, she slid off his back and stood weeping in the middle of the road, waiting for Jim.

Dr. Langdon sat on the end of Gee's bed and spoke to Emma and Jim, whom he had just called into the room.

"No bones broken, I'm glad to say. She's pretty badly bruised"—he laid his hand gently on the sheet over Gee's foot—"but basically she's intact." Turning his head, Dr. Langdon smiled at Gee, propped up on pillows. "She's a pretty tough old bird." Then, to Emma, "But your grandmother has had a serious setback. She wants me to level with you, Emma, and I have to tell you that this fall will very likely hasten the progress of her illness."

Emma said nothing. Next to her on the chaise longue under the window, Jim shifted and laid his hand briefly on her shoulder.

"On a practical level your grandmother will be greatly restricted in what she is able to do—in fact,

I've recommended that she get extra help in the house—"

"Not yet," Gee interrupted.

"—soon," Dr. Langdon continued.

Emma found her voice. "Gee, while Dr. Langdon is here, you know what I'm going to ask him—should we call Mom?"

"Not quite yet," Gee said, before the doctor could speak.

"I think we have to take one step at a time, Emma. No one knows exactly what each day will bring. I'm simply giving you the overall picture, to prepare you—the best I can, that is. No one really knows," he repeated.

"Why don't we call Dan and the girls and just tell them you've had a fall?" Jim suggested.

"Oh, *good* idea, Jim," said Emma. "If we could just do that, and tell them everything's under control . . ." What am I saying? she thought. I want Mom to come, I think.

"I don't see any reason not to do that. They'll probably call you, Hugh," said Gee to Doctor Langdon. "Will you handle their questions without going into the rest?" She put a hand to her head, clutching a fistful of hair, and spoke with passion. "I know, I know, I *know* I cannot let things slide much longer. But, please, give me a little more time. The moment I'm ready I will tell you. I promise."

At the beloved word, Emma felt a little crack in her heart.

From that day on a new aura enveloped Bell Brook Farm, affecting the rhythm of the place and touching, in varying degrees, the few who came and went.

Emma maintained her barn routine but discontinued the afternoon rides; the anxiety that attacked her periodically grew worse when Gee was out of sight, so that Emma even dreaded going to the barn. Instead, she stayed with Gee in the gardens, working among the flowers and vegetables under her grandmother's watchful eye.

When Joey called to ask her out, Emma explained to him, lowering her voice, that Gee had had a bad fall and could not be left. Joey came to call and offered to teach Emma how to drive, a project Gee heartily encouraged—"Now that we are virtually marooned here—even if you can't get your license until September."

But during the first lesson, Emma was so jittery about leaving her grandmother alone that she could not concentrate.

"Emma, what is the matter with you?" Joey asked, as they sat stalled in the middle of the orchard pasture. "She's sitting right up there in the garden, as snug as a bug in a rug. Now pay attention."

"Oh, Joey, I can't. That's just it, I *can't* pay attention!" said Emma and burst into tears.

Totally mystified, Joey tried to put his arms around her, but she pushed him away and jumped out of the car. That evening Emma called him to apologize.

"I'm sorry, Joey," she said. "Please be patient with me. Soon I'll try to explain how I feel, right now I can't . . . no, I won't go out with you for a while . . . when my Mom gets here. . . . Yes, oh, yes, then I'll go out with you."

To herself Emma said, I can't see Joey because I know I'd tell him, and I can't tell him because I will fall apart if I do.

Jim came, almost every day, after work. He came without papers, simply to sit with Gee while Emma did her evening barn chores. Often he stayed for supper, helping Emma cook the meal that only they ate, while Gee sipped broth and asked with lively interest about details of their day.

During one such evening, a week or so after her fall, she said to them, "I want to pack up my china. Will you help me? I want it all put away, inventoried—it'll make it easier later on."

For a moment Emma sat immobilized, held down by the weight in her chest. Then Jim rose and said, "Sure, Gee, where do you keep it all?" and Emma came to life again.

"There are the candlesticks in your room, Gee. I'll get them. And Jim, if you go into the Music Room, up on the top of the hutch you'll find the soup tureen. Be careful—the ladle's in it."

Gee started for the dining room. "I'll get the cups and saucers," she said. "Oh, Em, while you're in my room, don't forget those little figurines on the desk—the cow and the rooster."

"And the nut bowls—they're in the dining room, too," Emma reminded her, and to herself thought, How lighthearted she seems.

Soon the kitchen table was covered with all the bits and pieces of Gee's pink-and-white china. Emma got a sturdy carton from the cellar and tissue paper from the linen closet.

Gee picked up the pink-and-white cow. It was about five inches high; a rippled blue ribbon with a golden bell hanging from it circled the neck.

"Now this was the very first piece I found," she said. "Father's ship docked in Cherbourg and we had a whole week in Normandy before sailing home again. It was my first cruise, too, the first time I'd been away from home, and I felt very, very important....

"Well, I found the cow in a little china shop in St. Lô on our last day, and I remember thinking, I can't wait to show this to Mamie. It even made me impatient to get home again." She held the cow in the light. "Hardly what you'd call really fine workmanship, but pretty charming, don't you think?"

Emma said, "I love her. I've always loved the cow. She looks so wise, somehow."

"That sort of I-know-a-secret look on her face," said Jim, smiling at the cow. "What about the rooster, Gee?"

"Well, the rooster was much later, one of the last, actually. I found him in a yard sale right here in Vermont. But it's from the same foundry—look at the details, and the colors are identical, though who ever heard of a pink-and-white rooster?" And she cupped the rooster in both hands and kissed his comb.

"Well, whoever heard of a rooster reading a book, for heaven's sake," said Emma, and they all laughed, for indeed the little china rooster held a miniature blue notebook in one claw.

"Now, the cups," said Gee. "They were a real find...."

And so they passed the evening; hour after hour slipped by unnoticed as Gee told them stories about the pieces before wrapping them carefully in tissue paper and laying them in the carton.

The tureen she had found on her honeymoon.

Gee seldom spoke of her husband. He had died when they were both quite young, long before the girls started marrying, so none of the grandchildren knew him.

Now Emma asked her grandmother, "Where did you go on your honeymoon?"

"Well, Father was still a sea captain when I married your grandfather, and by now Mamie was going with him on his voyages. I suppose it sounds rather odd, but Father arranged for us to have the bridal suite on his ship. We sailed off with them— at least as far as Bermuda. They left us there for two weeks and picked us up on the way home."

Gee fell silent and Emma felt uncomfortable about stirring tender memories.

"I'm glad you asked, though, Em," said Gee. A happy smile lit her face. "We had a wonderful, wonderful time, your grandfather and I. It was a lovely honeymoon. And again, like the cow, it was on the last day in Bermuda that we found the tureen, just before sailing home again.

"It was sitting right in the middle of a shop window in Hamilton—a window that we had passed again and again without seeing it. When we went in the shopkeeper said he'd just put it in the window. Your grandfather bought it for me on the spot."

Again she smiled, widely, secretly, her eyes shining. "My word, we had fun," she said.

They had come to the end of the china.

Gee stood up and put her hand on Emma's head. "Now, darling," she said, "you may call your mother in the morning."

· · ·

Gee's daughters came, one by one, and her son, to see her and to make the necessary new household arrangements.

Promptly, wiping tears from her rosy face just once, Bertha said she would spend part of every day at Bell Brook Farm; the visiting nurse arranged to come every other day; friends and neighbors, hearing the news, put together a schedule for providing meals.

Pip got twenty-four-hour leave from the camp. Sonia Lunt went to meet his bus in Winslow. When Emma saw him swing off the seat of the Lunts' truck, she ran out of the Music Room door to talk to him before he came into the house.

"You didn't tell me it would move so fast," he said to her. "How long have you known?"

"Since she fell."

"Why didn't you write?"

"After you answered my letter, when I wrote you about the test results, I thought a lot about what you said—and I've been meaning and meaning to write back. But I just hate facing it all."

"Still, Em—"

"I know. I feel kind of bad about it now; you might have had more time with her."

"Not really, don't worry about that. I had trouble getting even twenty-four hours. You're only supposed to have the one long holiday break, but I explained it was an emergency. I didn't realize how much of a one it was, till Sonia told

me on the way out. It kind of took me by surprise."
He rubbed his forehead and squinted at Emma.
"Have you managed OK?"

"It's hard." Emma could feel her throat begin
to close. She swallowed. "Awfully hard. This is it,
Pip. Her time has come."

The dogs, having spied Pip through the screen
door, started to bark, and Pip and Emma moved
toward the house to silence them.

"Your time, too, Em. Remember, this is your
time, too."

"It helped a lot, you telling me that in your
letter. It helps now. I wish you could stay. Maybe
you could make this awful heavy ache go
away."

"No one can do that for you." They reached the
door and opened it and the dogs climbed Pip's
legs. "You've come this far all on your own." Pip's
voice faltered. Emma looked up at him and saw
that his eyes were damp. "I've only come to say
good-bye."

As soon as Joey heard that Nell had arrived at
Bell Brook Farm, he called Emma. "My mom says
your mom is here," he said. "And she told me why.
Can you get away for the evening?"

"Y-yes, I guess so." To Emma, Joey seemed to be
speaking from another life, a life in which it
mattered whether or not she agreed to be his girl.

How could it matter, when all that mattered was this dreadful heaviness inside her?

But when she ran down the lane that sultry evening, to meet him at the turn, she was glad to be going to Joey. At the sight of his car with the door hanging open for her, she hurried to him and climbed in.

Instead of making everything all right, as she had hoped, Joey only said, rather crossly, "Why didn't you tell me about your grandmother?"

Disappointed, Emma tried as well as she could to explain. She shivered slightly but continuously as she talked, until Joey interrupted her.

"Stop that, Emma, it's hot out."

She began to cry and he put his arms around her.

"Everything's so *different* now," she said, hiccoughing and wiping her nose on the cuff of her shirt.

"How long . . . ," Joey began.

"Not very. Not very long at all," said Emma, beginning to cry again. "And, oh, Joey, she's being so brave."

"Are you scared?"

"Yes, very."

"Me, too. Come on, let's get out of here, let's go to town. Forget the movies. Let's eat and then drive around."

"I told Mom I wouldn't be late. We could go

back to the farm after supper and sit in the sitting room."

"*No*," said Joey emphatically. "Come on, Emma, let's talk about something else."

They ate at Dino's. The change of scene whetted Emma's appetite; despite the midsummer heat wave, she ate with a nervous gusto, wolfing down slice after slice of pizza, without speaking to Joey.

In the pizza parlor he was more like himself, or at least more like the Joey Emma had begun to discover this summer. Then again maybe she was more like the self she remembered from so long ago. Conscious of his eyes upon her, welcoming the distraction, she finished her pizza, and when Joey reached for her hand, she let him hold it.

"Emma, let's go," he said huskily.

"Okay."

She knew he wanted to kiss her and decided that was okay, too; it might help lighten the mass in her chest.

As they were leaving Dino's, Lettie came in with her boyfriend. Immediately she took Emma in her arms, unmindful of the stares of the other diners or Joey's evident discomfort.

"Oh, Em," she whispered, hugging Emma tight. "Dear Em, I'm thinking of you all the time."

In the dark car, parked at the foot of the lane, Joey and Emma were locked in a sticky embrace. Emma broke away.

"It's no use, Joey. All I can think of is what's going on up at the house. I'm sorry."

And Emma really was sorry. She longed for the pleasure and release that her body had begun to enjoy when she was last with Joey.

"Take me home, please."

Willingly, Joey put the car in gear and drove up the lane. It was only nine o'clock, barely dark.

"Won't you come in and see Mom? Sukie's here, too. They'd love to see you."

"*No*," said Joey. Then, more gently, "No, Em, another time. Should I call?"

They both knew it was hopeless.

"Afterwards, Joey," Emma said. "Call me afterwards."

At Gee"s request, the family moved her bed downstairs, to the Music Room, and set it up in the big south window. She spent more and more time in it, watching the comings and goings in the house, relinquishing her reign to all who tended her.

Occasionally, she went to the garden, leaning heavily on a cane or someone's shoulder. Once she asked Libba to drive her down to the barn.

"I want to see how Yankee is coming along," she said.

Moved, and proud, too, Emma showed her grandmother how well the colt behaved on a lead line.

"What a *beautiful* job you have done, are doing, pumpkin. Never, ever, has this barn looked so organized and tidy, or all the animals so well. Even the geese," she added with a little laugh.

"I'm not afraid of them anymore," said Emma. She brandished a pitchfork at the approaching gander, and he retreated, mumbling darkly.

"Would you put Hal through his paces for me?" Gee sat down rather abruptly on a couple of hay bales and leaned back against the barn.

"You sure, Ma?" asked Libba.

"Very sure, Libba dear."

So Emma caught Hal and put on his tack and showed Gee how far he had come in his training. She made him yield to her leg and do his magnificent extended trot and she brought him to a square halt in front of Gee.

"I am impressed. Really impressed. Barely two months and you've got him ready to show. He'll be worth a fortune, at this rate, Em. He's just what every three-day-eventer wants, what with his jumping. . . ."

Her voice petered out, and Emma looked away. Neither of them could talk about the future of the horses.

Libba spoke up. "Come on, Ma, like it or not, I'm taking you back up. It's time for tea."

There came a time, a lull in the progress of the disease, when none of Gee's children was staying at Bell Brook Farm and Gee and Emma were alone together, with the exception of Bertha's daily ministrations and Jim's frequent visits.

He came one evening during this brief spell, as the early-August moon was waning, bringing strawberry ice cream, Gee's favorite. She asked for a little dish but after tasting it put it aside.

"How enigmatic the moon looks tonight, as she withdraws," said Gee. "Golden, too."

They all watched it hanging over the hills across Bell Brook valley, remote and indifferent in the vast, black, country sky. Emma turned to speak to Gee and found Jim's eyes upon her. Immediately he looked away.

Suddenly self-conscious, Emma forgot what she was going to say; she began to gather their bowls, the tinkle of spoons against glass loud in the quiet room.

As though to fill the awkward little void, Jim cleared his throat and said, "That song you like so much, Gee—Emma mentioned it at Mrs. Archer's picnic, something to do with the Navy? Anyway, I've been meaning to ask you to play it for me. Could we have it now?"

Emma jumped up, her hands full. "That's right! You've never heard it. Let's do play it now—I'll just take these into the kitchen."

In the semi-dark she stumbled slightly going up the steps, and Gee's ice cream slid out of its bowl onto the kitchen floor. Returning from the sink with a sponge, Emma heard her grandmother say in a voice that was new to Emma, a very private, very gentle voice:

"Good things are well worth waiting for."

And Jim answered very quietly, "I know. Truly I know. I—I—"

Well, that old song isn't *that* good, thought Emma to herself. Quickly she mopped up the melted ice cream, humming so that Gee and Jim would not think she was eavesdropping. But in the Music Room there was only silence, and Emma could not help wondering what Jim had been about to say.

Joining them again, she turned on the light near the stereo and searched through the basket where Gee kept all her tapes.

"That's funny, it's not here," she said in a puzzled voice.

"Oh, Em, what a shame. Now I remember—I lent it to Pip. He swore to send it back next week. No matter, Jim, it's just something of a family joke, really. Do look—" Gee pointed out the window. "See what that cloud does to the moon? How mysterious she looks?"

Jim rose to his feet, and he and Emma and Gee watched a silvery cloud drift across the golden moon.

"I should be off," he said, after a while. "Good night, Gee, Em. We'll play the song another time."

. . .

On the tenth of August, Gee took another turn for the worse. Her children returned, first one at a time, but soon all of them, as it became evident that Gee's time was near. Extra help was found, to spell the family sitting with her around the clock, and the visiting nurse came twice a day.

Emma took her turn with the rest. On the morning of the fourteenth she sat in the Music Room, watching her grandmother's face. By now the heaviness filled Emma until it seemed to push against her ribs, though she supposed it must have left room for her heart, for she could feel it beating somewhere.

Gee hardly spoke now. She lay with her eyes half-closed, her face remote.

Hoping to bring her grandmother back, yearning to hear the familiar voice, Emma leaned close to her and whispered, "It's me, Gee, me, Emma."

Gee turned her distant eyes on Emma's and held them for a long moment.

"Oh, Gee, you are being very brave," Emma said, her heart in pain.

"I am not being brave," Gee said suddenly, quite tartly, in an echo of her old voice. "I am busy. I am paying attention."

The next night, Gee said, from the shadows of her bed in the darkened room, "Nell, pack my bag. I want to go home."

After that she spoke to them not at all. It seemed

to the family that she did not even know that they were there, though sometimes she fixed half-open eyes on theirs.

On the morning of the sixteenth Emma relieved Pam. She held her grandmother's hand, which lay passive and waxy in hers, until Gee withdrew her hand and raised it in the air, palm upward, as though in supplication. Emma stood up and stepped back from the bed. What did Gee want? Emma thought her heart would break, so forsaken was the gesture.

The hand fell back of its own accord and Gee frowned, the lines deep in the colorless face. Her eyes were closed, but her face looked very focused, as though she were listening for a voice, a sign, a passage of music.

A moment later she raised both arms. She seemed to Emma to be reaching for something, searching. The arms lifted weakly and fell back and lifted yet again, restlessly, longingly. Emma gave a little cry and went to call her mother, but by the time she and Nell reurned to the Music Room, Gee lay still again.

All the next day nothing happened at Bell Brook Farm; nothing changed, not even the perfect weather. No phone rang, no visitors came; in the Music Room all was silence; silence reigned, silence and timelessness. The family spoke in whispers, if they spoke at all, and moved slowly through the old house, as though in a vacuum.

Late that evening Emma took her turn once more at the bedside. Gee still lay motionless and gray; no longer did she lift her arms in that restless searching fashion that had so wrung Emma's heart.

A lower corner of the sheet was turned up, and when Emma leaned over the bed to straighten it, she saw Gee's feet: they were blue. Frightened, Emma sat back in the chair.

The room, the whole house, was still—helpers departed, family resting, refrigerator subsided, and not a sound came from the barnyard.

Emma studied her grandmother's face. What was the expression upon it? Intent. Was that the word? And immediately Emma remembered Gee saying, "I am busy. I am paying attention." Yet how unfamiliar the face on the pillow looked, thought Emma sadly, drawn closed, so excluding, so forbidding in its inward concentration. What did Gee want to hear?

On and on Emma sat in the quiet shadowed room, until, despite herself, her lids began to grow heavy. Just as she gave in and let her head fall forward, a voice said, "Yes."

Emma sat bolt upright, her heart pounding, her mind and body vigilantly attentive. She said, "Yes," Emma thought, not believing it, but when

147

she looked at her grandmother she knew it was true. An expression of utter astonishment lit Gee's face.

Emma watched her without moving, hardly breathing. Suddenly her skin began to prickle and grow warm; at the same moment Gee opened her eyes and stared intently past Emma to a corner of the room. What did Gee see?

Emma turned and felt an extraordinary glow enter her body. Something had come into the room, something she could not see, or call by name, but Gee saw it. Gee knew. Emma knew Gee knew. Emma knew that what Gee had been yearning for had come.

Gee opened her eyes wider and watched it approach the bed, and once again, slowly, and surely this time, she raised her arms and opened them in greeting.

"Yes," she said, her eyes wide with wonder. "Yes."

And then, in the next moment, Emma knew that whatever it was had left and that Gee had gone with it. For a little while she sat with her grandmother's hand in hers and felt the pulse, steady but weaker now. Then she got up and went to the door and called her mother, who had fallen asleep with her head on the kitchen table.

"It's time," Emma said. "You'd better fetch the others."

Nell roused her sisters and brother; one by one

they filed into the Music Room and sat with Gee, around her bed, watching her breathe, slower and slower. For over an hour they sat, until the breathing stopped.

"It's over," said Nell. "She has died."

But Emma knew that Gee had already left them a while ago.

When the undertakers from Winslow had come to take Gee's body away and, finally, the family parted to sleep what was left of the night, Emma went to her room and undressed by the light of the stars.

She felt numb, all sensation muffled. Automatically she went into the bathroom she used to share with Gee, automatically she brushed her teeth, washed her face, which—as she splashed water over it did not even feel like hers—and automatically slipped on her nightgown.

On her way out she paused and looked at the mural, and when her eye fell on the place where the colt had been and no longer was, her heart wrenched, piercing the numbness. Then she turned out the orange sun and went back to her room and got into bed. Not for a moment did she expect to sleep. She really did not know what to expect.

To her surprise drowsiness began to overtake her as soon as she turned on her side. Gratefully she lent herself to it.

How tired I am, she thought, letting herself

down, down into sleep. At the very last moment her heart skipped a long beat, and she held her breath.

In her ear a voice murmured, Dearest pumpkin, good night.

At the two *p*s of "pumpkin," breath stirred a wisp of her hair; and on the top of her head, so light and so swift that she wondered if she had imagined it, Emma felt the touch of a hand.

"Gee?" she whispered, sitting up in the bed. She stared around the dim little room, searching, but the only thing that moved was a curtain at her open window. So Emma lay down again and fell instantly asleep.

PART THREE

E mma, it's Joey."
   "Hi, Joey."
Emma sat on the telephone stool in the front
hall, her feet plaited through its legs, one elbow
propped against the wall. It was six days later.

"How're you doing?"

"Okay, I guess. We've all been awfully busy.
There's so much to attend to."

"Who's 'we'?"

"Well, Mom's gone home, but two of the aunts
are staying on this week—Pam and Lexy. Then
they go Wednesday and Sukie and Libba come
back. . . ."

"And you? You going to stay on?"

"Of course; I'll be here until the end."

"The end of what?"

"The end of the summer."

"You mean through Labor Day? Through your
birthday?"

"Yup. We all decided Gee would've wanted to
have that party just like she planned" (In her
head Emma could hear Gee: "as, just *as* we
planned" and Emma smiled) "—friends, neigh-

bors, and the family, of course—they're all coming back. You're invited, Joey. It's also a party for her, for Gee."

"God, Em, that's great you're going to be here another two weeks almost—Labor Day's late this year—"

"Eleven days, actually. School starts the Wednesday after Labor Day, so Mom and Pop'll have to drive straight through to make it." I'll be sixteen, Emma thought, but the fact did not move her as once it had; she had too much else on her mind. Before she turned sixteen she had to find homes for all those horses. She sighed into the phone.

"Listen, Em, a new pizza place just opened, down in Ludlum. How about I pick you up tonight and we'll give it a try? Then, if we want, we can take in the late show in Winslow. . . ."

Joey's voice trailed off and Emma remained silent, thinking: He never came at the end, never came near us; he was too afraid. But immediately she remembered how afraid she had been, and she felt contrite.

"Sure, Joey," she said into the phone. "Sure. I'd love to," although her heart sank a little. A part of her didn't want to spend even one evening away from Bell Brook Farm. "What time?"

Joey's voice was filled with delight. "I'll come get you at six," he said. "Be ready."

Emma hung up and went back to the Music

Room where Pam and Lexy were wrapping Gee's books in newspaper and putting them in the big storage cartons that the moving company had provided.

"Joey?" asked Lexy.

"Joey," Emma answered. "I told him I'd go out with him tonight."

Pam gave a little grunt of laughter. "You don't sound too thrilled."

"I just haven't had time to think about Joey."

"I know, Em." Pam swung her heavy hair back over her shoulder and smiled at Emma. "I'm glad you're going out with him. That's what you *should* be doing, not"—she gestured with one dirty hand at the dismembered room—"this; especially not on top of all the barn work." Pam looked at the cartons stacked around them. "I'll be glad when the others get here. Be sure to send Sukie straight to the garden. It needs her expert hand."

Lexy said, "You know what let's do, it's so nice out? Let's finish the books and make a picnic lunch and take it up to the ten-acre lot." Lexy ran her long, nervous fingers through her hair, just like Gee.

It was indeed a lovely day. No one could remember a summer to equal this one for weather. With the exception of the big storm, one perfect day succeeded another, week in, week out. Rain fell at night in just the right amount to keep the crops and flowers and vegetables growing lustily. For the first time in fifteen years, John Lunt told the aunts, he was going to get a third cutting of hay off the big south meadow.

Up at the ten-acre lot, lying on their backs, Lexy and Pam and Emma watched a pair of killdeer darting through the bottomless blue sky.

"How they squeal," said Lexy drowsily. "It's as though they didn't want us to relax."

"I remember when Gee first pointed them out to me," said Emma. "I couldn't get over the name. It's funny the way they love to be in the pastures with the horses."

"Do you miss her horribly?" asked Pam, curling sideways around her big belly to look at Emma.

"Yes." Emma was afraid she was going to cry. She waited a moment to regain control of her voice, then asked, "Don't you?"

"Yes, but it's different for all of us, being married, with families of our own. Even for Dan. First of all, he's in love; second, he's well into his own career. It must be hell for you, especially after this summer together. You were very brave to stay on, Emma. I should think it would make it much harder."

"I never even thought twice about it," said Emma. "I couldn't just leave—the project, all those animals . . . I *couldn't* leave Bell Brook Farm."

Again she felt her throat begin to close, and they all fell silent.

"That Jim Fothergill has done a great job for us," said Lexy. "Putting the place on hold, as it were."

"Yes. And those friends of his—young Dr. Beach and his wife—I like their looks. Imagine them just dropping out of the sky like that, just when we needed them. I'm sure they'll be good tenants." Pam stretched. "I suppose we ought to get back if we're *ever* going to get all that stuff packed up."

"I just wish they liked horses," said Emma, sitting up.

"Well, look at it this way, Em; at least this way we can store everything in the barn for the next few years."

"I wonder who'll end up here," said Emma. She gazed down at her beloved barnyard far below, just able to make out the geese as they waddled toward the maple and its generous dark shade.

"Who knows? Anything can happen in five years," said Lexy. "Maybe you, Em!"

Emma smiled. "Talk about dreams coming true," she said. She got to her feet and collected their paper cups. "Now if we can just settle the animals as nicely as the place, we'll really be in luck. I guess."

After her bath Emma spent several minutes rummaging through her drawers and closet, trying to decide what to wear for her date with Joey. It was hard to concentrate. Clothes had never meant a great deal to her. This summer she had lived in blue jeans, and for the past six days—only *six*, Emma marveled, hardly able to believe the glacial passage of time—she could not have said what she was wearing at any given moment, had anyone asked. Taking trouble over her dress was the only way Emma could get herself in a frame of mind to leave Bell Brook Farm at all. Except for the brief services at the church and cemetery, this would be the first time she had done so since Gee's death.

Finally, impatiently, she chose a clean denim skirt and a pretty checked shirt and slipped her narrow brown feet into leather thongs.

Joey arrived on the dot of six. Once out of the car, he stood awkwardly on the edge of the lawn, not quite able to meet Pam's eye when she called to him in greeting from the Music Room door.

Emma, coming up behind her aunt, muttered, "You might think he'd never seen you before and had heard you bite."

Pam turned her head so that Joey could not hear and said, "He's just shy, scared to see us for the first time since Ma died. People often are."

"I know, I know." Emma brushed crossly past Pam and out the door. "Hi, Joey," she said.

Bit by bit conversation between them became easier as they sat in the new pizza parlor in Ludlum, trading slices and passing judgment on them.

"I think Dino's crust is better," said Emma. "But I love the cheese they use here. It's different." Emma was pleased to note that she really was interested in the pizza, and even glad she had agreed to go out with Joey. Bell Brook Farm was not the same with another generation present, all women with more authority than hers.

The more relaxed Emma became, the more Joey blossomed. Soon he was telling her anecdotes about his work with Ray Flanagan; he even succeeded in making her laugh.

Finally Joey asked, "What's going to happen to the farm, Em? Will you be coming back next year?"

With a ripple of the pain that she assumed would never go away, Emma told him about the new tenants.

"Gee's lawyer found them. The man's just out of medical school and his wife's a nurse and they're coming to work in Winslow. He's going to be Dr. Langdon's assistant for the next few years, while they decide if they want to settle here for good. Mom and the aunts think it's a perfect solution, and I guess it is." It *is*, dummy, you know it is. Otherwise we might lose the farm. "But the hitch is, they don't want to take on the animals. I mean they don't ride, so you can hardly expect them to look afer all those horses. . . ." I sound just like Mom, she thought sourly.

"So what are you all going to do about them?"

"It's not 'us all,' it's *me*. They've left it up to me to figure out. Oh, let's not talk about it, Joey."

"Okay. How about another coke? Ice cream?"

But talking about the farm had made Emma restless and she asked if they could go. Joey, sensing his mistake, was wise enough to leave her alone.

When they arrived at the foot of Gee's lane, he stopped the car, with the motor running, and before Emma could protest, he said to her, "I'm sorry about your grandmother, Emma, truly I am. And I feel bad about not coming to see any of you before she died. Some time I'd like to talk to you about it. But not now." He cupped his hand under her chin and turned her head to face him. "Please, Emma, will you go out with me again? Day after tomorrow?"

And Emma, touched, said yes.

By the end of the following day the books and ornaments and pictures in the Music Room were all packed and ready to go to the barn when the movers came to empty the house for the new tenants.

"We're making very good progress," Lexy pronounced wearily, as she came into the kitchen.

Emma, smudged with dirt and lightly coated with hay chaff, sat at the kitchen table. She hated having the beloved room stripped, hated seeing all her private little treasures in the house put away.

It just blots Gee out, she thought; and, like a child digging fingernails into flesh to ward off a doctor's needle, she thumped her chest, hard, to dull the pain in her heart.

"What are we having for supper, Pammo?" Emma asked, watching Pam peel tomatoes.

"Jim Fothergill's coming out, so I thought I'd make a really good sauce from scratch and put it over the rest of that chicken Lexy and I had last night . . . while you were out carousing in the fleshpots of Ludlum."

Emma smiled. "Jim likes chicken," she said, a little possessively, rather taken aback to discover how pleased she was that he was coming. She wondered what it would be like to have him there, without Gee, with the aunts, whom he barely knew. Pam and Jim were about the same age, Emma realized, hoping she would not feel too left out.

For there was no doubt about it: Above and beyond the fundamental change at Bell Brook Farm, it was different with the aunts around; even having her mother there had caused mixed feelings in Emma, so long had she been Gee's ally, so long coped on her own. In a way it was a relief not to have all the responsibility, and in a way it was a shock.

What do they know? she asked herself defiantly

from time to time, when they talked about how Gee would have liked things done; they don't even put the spoons back in the right place.

On the whole, however, it was comforting to have them there. Different. But then everything was different.

Thinking the word, something stirred in Emma. Different empty, different sad. But different in another, important way, too. How? How different?

"Emma, where's Ma's china, do you know? I suddenly realized the tureen wasn't on the big hutch in there—" Lexy nodded in the direction of the Music Room—"and then I saw that none of it is around."

"No, it's all packed away. I told Mom when she was here and she probably forgot to tell you—Jim and Gee and I wrapped it up the night Gee said I could call Mom and tell her she was sick." Emma was quite sure she would never forget that night.

She got up. "I'm going up to take a bath. I'll set the table when I come down."

"Hey! Let's eat in the dining room," said Lexy. "And *I'll* set the table, if you like, Em, and we'll have candles and real napkins."

Emma went over to her aunt and put her arms around her.

"That'll be nice, Lexy. Real nice."

. . .

"The last time I sat at this table you told me what to expect at Mrs. Archer's picnic," said Jim, smiling at Emma. "Especially the sparklers."

"Yes." Suddenly Emma felt shy, a child among adults.

"We had chicken that night, too, didn't we, Emma?" Jim asked her. He turned to Pam and Lexy. "Your mother fixed us an elegant meal. She had on that long dress, and she looked beautiful." To Emma again: "Didn't she?"

Emma nodded.

"What did she do to that chicken? Didn't it have ginger in it?"

Emma looked up. "Yes—good for you, Jim. It was her secret chicken—ginger and brandy and mint."

Pam and Lexy laughed.

"Oh, we know that one well," said Pam.

"Whenever Ma found a dish everyone liked— and quite often she invented them—she'd serve it six or eight times in a row, until everyone was sick of it, including her," Lexy told Jim. "It always tasted good the first time."

"Well, this is awfully good, too," he said.

From the corner of her eye Emma watched him cut another bite of Pam's casserole. In the candle-light his thick dark hair glinted, the curls forced behind his ears.

"Jim, you can't imagine how grateful we all

are to you—for everything," said Pam, a little formally.

"Oh, come on, Pam, any lawyer would have done the same." He looked at her. "But, you see, also, I loved her," he added simply.

The two sisters and Emma's eyes filled with tears. Quickly Pam said, "You do know about Emma's birthday party, don't you? Of course you do. Well, we're still going to have it—a sort of combination birthday-memorial-farewell. . . ." Her voice faltered. "Oh, dear, *not* a good idea, to bring it up just now. Good grief, what a lachrymose party this is turning into." She wiped her eyes and laughed a little huskily, and Lexy joined her. Even Emma managed to smile.

"Let's go back to talking about food," Emma said. "What do you think we should serve at the Labor Day party, Jim?"

Jim put down his knife and fork and took a pad of paper and a pencil out of his breast pocket. "Okay. Let's see," he said, starting to write. "Cold ham?"

"Vegetable salad," said Pam.

"Yes, and one hot dish," Lexy added.

"Gee's secret chicken!" they all said at once, and for the rest of the dinner they elaborated on the feast they would prepare for Emma's birthday party.

"Because that's what it really is, mostly," said Pam.

. . .

After coffee Emma said, "There's a sick kitten in the barn; I'm just going to nip down to check it."

"Why don't I come, too?" Jim suggested. "Let's do the dishes first."

"Nonsense, Jim, you're our guest, and this is our job, anyway. Go on, go with Emma . . . here, honey, take the flashlight"—Lexy thrust it into Emma's hand. "You'll need it, there's no moon."

Lexy was right. They did need the flashlight, for clouds had covered the stars and darkened the sky.

"We'll get a shower tonight," said Emma. "A long one, I hope. We're beginning to need another."

The beam of the flashlight swung back and forth like a pendulum as they walked down to the barn. When Emma opened the door to the lower level and they went inside, it was like stepping into a separate little secret world.

Because of the kitten, Emma had turned on the heating lamp that hung at the end of a long string over one of the lambing pens. Its warm orange light shed a conical glow onto the invalid curled in its box of hay underneath the lamp. No other light showed in the damp dark barn.

Emma knelt beside the box and picked up the kitten.

"What do you think?" she asked.

Jim took the kitten in one hand, curling his long

fingers gently around it; with the other he stroked the top of the kitten's head.

"Looks okay to me," he said. "How was it before?"

"Very down-in-the-mouth."

Just then the kitten opened its mouth, startlingly pink, baring pinprick teeth, and gave a contented and surprisingly loud meow.

Jim and Emma laughed.

"Hold it a sec, will you, Jim, and we'll try some milk."

She jumped up and felt her way to the feed room to fetch the little bowl she had set aside. Returning to the lambing pen, she sat cross-legged in the pyramid of light and dipped her finger in the milk. The kitten sucked it hungrily. Drop by drop it drank its way through half the bowl; then Jim set it on its feet, and Emma put the bowl in front of it, and while they watched, it finished off all the milk.

"So much for that crisis," said Emma, settling the kitten back in its box.

"Would that they all turned out so well." Jim leaned back against the wooden partition and stretched out his long legs so that they were the only part of him visible in the orange light. From the surrounding dark, he said, "It's so peaceful here. . . . I hate to bring it up, but have you gotten any further about the animals? I feel especially responsible as Doc and Nonie are friends of mine."

"Well, the fact is, Jim, that no one will take on the whole shebang. Horses need constant work—I realize that. When they're not your own, it's not the same. . . . I don't mind so much about selling the sheep and, God knows, the geese"—she snorted—"I don't mind a *bit* about them, and I expect the cats will stay on. And Mom says we can take Dumbo and old Witch home with us. But the horses . . ."

They sat without speaking for a while, Emma with her head bent over the box, watching the kitten lick its paws.

"I can't even begin to sort them out. The only thing I know for sure is that Hal's worth quite a lot of money, so I guess I'll just pull myself together and put ads in the horse journals this week. In fact he's so good I bet he'll go out of state."

"Why don't you wait a bit," said Jim. "Let me think some more, too. What about the others?"

"That's just it. . . ." Emma realized she was beginning to sound tearful, so she held her tongue until the moment passed and kept her head down. "Who on earth would take old Ben and Mrs. Tig? And they're nowhere near doddering enough to put to sleep."

"You haven't had an awful lot of time, Em, and you've still got almost ten days. . . ."

"The young pony's easier—to part with and also to place," Emma went on. "It's a shame to have to give him up, but now that all the kids won't be coming up to ride in the summer . . . anyway I'll ask around and find someone who'll be glad to take him."

"And that leaves Chloe and Yankee."

"Exactly. That leaves Chloe and Yankee."

"Well, let's not talk about it anymore now. We'll figure something out."

Emma looked up and spoke to where she could just make out Jim's face. "The only thing we've got to figure out is how I'm going to be able to stand giving up these horses." Then she made a little face and smiled a clown's smile. "Boo hoo, poor me."

"Emma, I wanted to talk to you about something else—the party—"

"You know," Emma interrupted him. "That is something to look forward to. It's sad in one way, of course, but good, too, having a party like that, to help mark the end of one time and the beginning of a new time. I'm glad you'll be here—"

"That's just it, Em, I didn't want to bring it up at dinner until I'd had a chance to talk to you alone, but I have to go to Africa—"

"To *Africa?* For Labor Day?"

"The firm in New York has arranged for me to go the Monday before Labor Day for a week or ten days. I tried to get them to switch it to the following week, but no go."

"Oh, dear." Emma's face resumed its woebegone look. "It just doesn't seem right, you not being here, for Gee, if not for me."

"I mind for both," said Jim quietly.

"Well, this has been some summer," said Emma. "I guess we'd better go back up to the house." She stood up and held out her hand to Jim. "Come on."

He grasped it, and Emma pulled him to his feet. Before letting go Jim's hand, Emma said, "Thank you for telling me first. It makes me feel kind of . . . oh, I don't know—grown-up, I guess, or special."

Jim opened his mouth and closed it again; side by side they left the barn and walked back up to the house, the errant pale beam leading the way.

The next afternoon, halfway through her self-imposed task of sorting all the tack into keep, sell, and give-away piles, Emma remembered she had promised to go out with Joey that evening.

Something inside her rebelled. Wondering what it could be, Emma set down the bridle she was holding and, on sudden impulse, climbed the ladder to the loft. In a way it seemed as though she had stepped backward in time, so clearly did she remember her musings that first evening at Bell Brook Farm. It was like coming upon a familiar suit of clothes that she had lost track of somewhere along the way and donned again with a certain unexpected delight. The hayloft was full now and almost overpowering in its rich sweet smell. Emma sat down.

Now why don't I want to go out with Joey? she asked herself. It's not Gee, it's not leaving the farm for a few hours, it's not even Joey himself.

The child inside her began to kick up a fuss again, and Emma smiled. You know what, she said to the child after a while; you and I are going to have one last glorious ride, just you and me and Hal. Then I'll go out with Joey and we'll see. . . .

At two o'clock Emma rode by the house, heading west on Hal. She waved to Pam and Lexy, who sat on the front steps packing glasses in the sun; they looked up as though to hail her, but Emma kept going.

At half past five, Lexy and Pam heard the slow clip-clop of a horse's feet in the lane. They ran together to the front door and were standing on the steps when Emma rode Hal up the rise.

"Where *have* you been, Emma?" Lexy called to her. "We were getting worried." Nervously, she twisted her wedding ring around and around.

"You needn't have," said Emma, drawing to a halt. "Hal and I just had the most wonderful ride in the world. It was our last one, you see. From now on I'm going to help you all close up the house and get ready for the party; after chores, that is." She nudged the weary horse with her legs.

"I've got to keep moving. Joey's picking me up at six-thirty, and I want to have a bath first."

Halfway down the slope to the barn, Emma turned in the saddle and called, *"Pam!"*

Pam, who was just letting the screen door close behind her, poked her head out. "What?"

"Can I borrow that green shirt of yours and the beads I like?"

Pam smiled. "Sure," she said. "You bet, Em."

Coming out of the theater at ten o'clock that evening, Emma felt thoroughly discombobulated. For the past two hours she and Joey had sat through the main feature, supposedly paying attention to it, while at the same time Joey made subtle but persistent love to her, thereby distracting Emma to the point where she could not even remember the name of the film.

Her eyes watched the screen, her ears heard pieces of the dialogue and most of the background music, but—her mind having apparently evaporated into the darkened theater—every bit of the rest of her throbbed to Joey's touch.

It started with his holding her hand; then he'd draped an arm over the back of her seat, finally curling it around Emma's shoulders; gently—tantalizingly—he stroked her bare arm. It wasn't until near the end of the movie that he began to kiss her, lavishly, by which time Emma was in a storm of impatience and far more enthusiastic than she had been before.

She sensed that the dark surroundings and pretended concentration on the screen had quickened her response, but what a welcome change it made from the past long weeks, this purely physical and quite delicious abandon. Joey was both gentle and ardent; quite talented, too, she decided, at this intoxicating game.

The question is, how much do I want to play?

If the past two hours were any measure, a great deal, said her body. Once out on the familiar streets of Winslow, however, the fever ebbed somewhat, and her mind, which on leaving the theater had been miraculously restored to her and was functioning again—albeit somewhat erratically—said, go easy.

Deciding to play for more time, Emma said, "Let's have ice cream."

"Fine by me," said Joey, distinctly pink and flushed and looking, thought Emma, just a little too much like the cat that swallowed the canary. Here, in her fog, Gee's face floated before her mind's eye, the evening her grandmother stood in the Music Room and held out her hand for the present Emma had brought. You look like the cat that swallowed the canary, Gee had said. I must write Pip to bring the tape back when he comes for Labor Day. Emma's mind continued to career around and around. Then, focusing once more on Joey: My word, I wonder if I'm pink, too.

"What?" She found they had arrived at Farley's Drug Store and Ice Cream Parlor and that Joey was waiting for some sort reply.

"I said, you want a frappe or a soda?" Joey asked.

Emma pulled herself together. "A chocolate malted frappe, please. Double on the chocolate."

They sat in silence, in a booth, Joey as grateful as she, Emma suspected, for this respite in the cosy old-fashioned drugstore. Rolling the thick, creamy, rich confection around her mouth to warm it up before swallowing, Emma was reminded of all the summers of her childhood. Just as she finished the frappe and was tilting her glass to suck the last few drops from the bottom, Joey cleared his throat.

Oh, dear, Emma thought, he's going to ask me where we stand, and I don't know.

She looked at Joey, at his bony, friendly, familiar face, clean-shaven, no longer a boy's face, nor yet a man's.

I just don't know.

"Was it bad, at the end?" Joey asked.

Emma, caught up in replaying the action in the theater, was startled. "What?"

"Your grandmother—"

"Oh, you mean when Gee died." Immediately, and as completely as though she had been bodily transported back to Bell Brook Farm, Emma resumed her summer self.

"Yeah," said Joey.

Emma thought about it. "No. Not really. Not at the end."

"I just couldn't . . ."

Rather sadly bidding farewell to her preoccupation with their amorous play, Emma turned her attention to making Joey feel better. As she did so, she felt herself drawing further and further away from him.

"I know, Joey. I understand. I probably couldn't have come to you, either, if it'd been your family. People are scared of death."

All at once their sensual encounter in the darkened movie theater seemed merely a diversion from the demands of real life. Too bad. She might well have played a little more with Joey. Now the mood had passed.

"My mother says you were with her when she died. I don't see how you did it."

"It was . . ." Her voice trailed off; once again she sat by Gee's bed and saw the look of wonder on her face.

"You don't have to talk about it," Joey said hastily.

How *could* I talk about that, to you? How could you understand? I don't really understand, myself. I only know something is different since she died. Something special, Emma thought. She felt years older than Joey, whole milestones ahead of him in life.

When Joey stopped the car at the foot of the lane and turned to take her in his arms, Emma was unable to summon her earlier passion, nor did she want to.

Not now, she sighed inwardly, trying to respond to Joey's lips upon hers. Poor Joey, it's not his fault.

"Maybe another time," Emma murmured. Gently she extricated herself from Joey's embrace, gently she kissed him good night.

"It's as though you know something I don't know," Joey whispered.

Perhaps I do, thought Emma. I wish I could be sure.

To Joey she said, "I just don't know how to talk about it yet. I'm going to walk home now. Thank you, Joey."

When his car disappeared down the dark little country road, Emma started up the lane. Gratefully she allowed the farm to enfold her.

No rain again, she thought absently. Oh, look, the moon—Pip was right. Twice it has been full before my birthday.

In the distance, at the top of the rise, Emma could see the upstairs windows lit and inviting.

Bed, she thought and, craving it, hastened her pace.

Suddenly her bones ached from the long afternoon ride. No other sensation moved her, just the deep, welcome fatigue, and a lingering memory of how good her frappe had tasted.

"Emma, I've come to say good-bye." Jim appeared in the barn door just as Emma finished her morning chores. She set down the pail she was carrying. "Oh."

"And also to tell you some good news about the horses," said Jim.

Once inside the barn, out of the sun's glare, Emma could see him more clearly. He was dressed in his city clothes.

"Well, almost any news about them would be good news. Except for selling the pony, I'm not getting anywhere."

"Ah, but I am." Jim grinned.

"You look like the cat that swallowed the canary," Emma said and laughed a little.

"Just listen to this: one, I met this guy—he lives in Ludlum—who wants to buy Hal. He wants to show him—eventing, mostly—for the next few years. If he ever decides to sell him, he'll give you first refusal."

"Jim, that's wonderful. I hated having him go out of state."

"And he says you can ride Hal any time you come back to Vermont."

"Well, that's nice, too, but I don't see how I ever will—not for five years, anyway."

"Two," Jim continued, "Lettie, your friend and now mine, Lettie Reynolds knows someone who'd love to have Mrs. Tiggywinkle. They're a really nice family—I've been to see them—with one little girl who is beside herself with joy to have a pony. *And* they'll take old Ben, just to keep Mrs. Tig company."

Emma's eyes filled with tears. "Oh, Jim," she said. "Why on earth didn't I think of Lettie?"

"God knows, my dear girl, it's just lucky someone did, because—and I want you to sit down." He laid his hands on Emma's shoulders and pressed her firmly down onto a hay bale. "Because, Emma, number three, *Lettie wants to buy Chloe.* Apparently she's always admired her. Lettie's going to start giving riding lessons next summer, and she needs another good horse."

Emma swallowed. "And . . . and . . . Yankee?" she whispered.

" 'And Yankee?' " Jim looked down at her, smiling. "Four: Lettie will take Yankee. She called your mother in Wheeling last night—just as your parents were leaving to come back up here—and they agreed to pay his board until you're ready to take him over yourself."

Without making any sound, Emma started to cry. Big salty tears ran around her cheekbones and down onto her neck. Jim squatted beside her. He put one hand behind her head and laid it on his shoulder.

"Hey," he said. "You're supposed to be happy."

"I am," Emma wept. "I am happy, Jim. It's the most perfect arrangement I ever heard. It's just...." She hiccoughed. "Now it's all so final. It's all over." She struggled with her voice. "It's just that I'll miss them. You see, I like to take care of things...."

Always have, she thought, and an image appeared in her mind of herself, at the age of six, sitting in the bathtub, unwilling to hold her washcloth under water, for fear that it would drown.

"Oh, Em," said Jim into her hair.

For a minute Emma thought he was going to cry, too. She pulled herself together.

"Thank you, Jim, it's really too good to be true."

Jim sat back on his heels. "Lettie's going to ask you if you want to work for her, if she makes a go of the riding school. In a year or two she's going to need more horses, and someone to help her in the summers."

"Oh, well, a year or two—that's a long time."

"Think about it," said Jim.

"I don't know how I'd feel about being in Vermont and not at Bell Brook Farm."

"Well, in five years, maybe you will be."

"Five years is forever."

"No. No, it is not," Jim said very firmly. He took her hands in his. "Five years is not forever, Emma, it's just around the corner."

And in a little part of her mind, right near the center, Emma knew that this was true. She sighed. "I wish you could be at the party," she said.

"Me, too, Em."

"When do you get back?"

"A week from Thursday."

"And we leave Monday night. I hate good-byes."

"Me, too."

Emma looked into the kind hazel eyes. They were brushed with sadness, but behind the sadness Emma sensed something else. What was it? She could not quite decide.

"Will it be interesting, this case in Africa?" she asked.

Jim smiled. "Oh, yes. Very. I've never been to Africa."

"Me neither. I'd like to go, sometime, to see the animals."

"Yes," said Jim.

Emma realized her hands were still in his. As once before, she stood up and pulled him to his feet. "Come have coffee," she said.

"No, I must go. I've got meetings in New York for a couple of days before Africa—the first one's this afternoon."

Neither of them spoke for several moments. Then Jim said, "It looks as though I'll be in Wheeling about the third week of November. I'll call."

"Good," said Emma, looking up at him, thinking absently: November? Even November seems a long time away, another world, West Virginia, another life. "Good-bye, Jim," she said sadly.

When he leaned down to kiss her cheek, Emma remembered what it was about his eyes: They were very, very patient.

For the rest of that week Emma was so caught up in getting ready to leave and in helping her mother and the aunts prepare for the Labor Day celebration that she didn't have time to be sorry about Jim missing it, didn't think about him at all, except in a roundabout way, when it came time to empty the barn. In one fell swoop it happened— horses, sheep, even the geese, were gone. Only the half-wild cats remained.

Up at the house, however, it was almost like old times at Bell Brook Farm, as Emma's birthday approached. Clump by clump the whole family came, squeezing into the house, children sleeping three and four to a room. Even Cousin Horace had to share the guest room with Pip, because Pip's room had been taken over by his and Emma's parents. Only Emma slept alone.

Dear little room, she whispered, as she tumbled exhausted into bed the night before the party, I knew I was right to keep you.

Even the tree house was occupied. The next tier

of grandchildren had claimed it. After much ado and transportation of bedding and snacks, four little boys were out there now.

What fun for them, Emma thought, drowsily, remembering what it had been like to sleep out in the tree house when she was a child, remembering, too, that she had planned, so long, long ago, to spend tonight there. And on the very edge of sleep, she thought once more: Tomorrow is my last day at Bell Brook Farm.

"Happy birthday, darling."

Emma heard her mother's voice through a sweet morning mist of sleep. She rolled over and opened her eyes. Nell was sitting on the edge of her bed, bending over her.

"Hi, Mom," said Emma. "Is everyone up?"

"Everyone's up. The day has begun," said Nell. She grunted. "As a matter of fact the day began rather early. The tree-house gang, chickenhearted to a man, came in at two o'clock because they heard a barred owl right above them. So that woke Dumbo up, which woke Witch up, which woke the babies up—well, you get the picture. Eventually everyone got back to sleep again." Nell stood up and went to Emma's window. "Another perfect day," she said. "The weather man, this morning on the radio, said rain tomorrow, rain all this week, but today will hold. It will be the last perfect day of summer." Nell turned. "I see you've got all your things together, so it shouldn't take you too long to get ready when the party's over. Pop wants to leave by six."

"Yup," said Emma. "I'll be ready."

When her mother left the room, Emma got up very slowly and very slowly dressed herself in the clothes she had laid out the night before. Then she checked her two bags and tried once more, unsuccessfully, to close her trunk. I'll get Pip to do it, she thought.

Seeing her journal on the desk, she picked it up with the idea of sliding it under the top layer of clothes in the trunk. It fell open; idly Emma flipped through the pages, paused at random, and began to read:

June 24

AM   After chores finished reassembling bridle for pony. Used Chloe's cheek straps and Mrs. Tig's old snaffle. Remember to explain to Gee.

Called Mr. Nelson at Ludlum Supply to cut back on grain order. Grass holding fine. Mr. Nelson says Gee used 600 lbs. of 10-10-10 on orchard pasture May 28th, OK to use it now. (That's lucky, because Gee put horses in it last week.)

Checked slight abrasion on Ben's off front fetlock. How did he get it? Watch for infection.

New lamb followed me instead of her mother

*when I let them out to clean the pen. Remember to ask Gee when I can turn them out with rest of sheep.**

Worked Hal ½ hour only, pony ½ hour.

Lunch.

**Gee says next Tuesday. Mark date on calendar in barn.*

Sometimes I forget all about that letter, just put it out of my head. Is this wrong? It doesn't feel wrong, but writing it down makes it seem wrong—to forget, to pretend. Does Gee pretend? Does she think about it all the time? Maybe it's not wrong because she seems OK, inside and out, and so does the house and the barn and the whole place seem OK, like the garden, it's never been more beautiful. Maybe it's the weather ...

PM Rode Hal up the old brook road to the birch forest. He is going much better on the trails, spooks less....

Another world, Emma thought to herself, another life. She turned several pages and read :

No sign of mouse all week. Where can he have gone?

Ben's abrasion has healed completely. Remember to tell Gee to buy more Bag Balm next time we go to Winslow.

Flock has accepted ewe and lamb, no sweat.
Hal still won't do a square halt right. I
must . . .

How unimportant it all sounds. Should I even bother to pull it together for the judges? So much editing . . .

She let the journal fall shut and knelt down to tuck it in the trunk.

All those people downstairs—my family—waiting to say happy birthday to me, but also good-bye Bell Brook Farm, good-bye Gee.

Tears stung her eyes.

I wish my heart didn't feel so *sore*, said Emma to herself, rising and going to the mirror.

She peered at herself, rubbed at her eyes, and brushed her hair.

"Cheer up," she said to her reflection in the glass. "It's your birthday."

Although stripped of all its pictures and ornaments, the old house at Bell Brook Farm retained its charm. Sunlit, elegant, it welcomed all. In the dining room Dr. Langdon's wife stood talking to Sukie.

"You girls have done a lovely job. Gee would be proud of you. The food's delicious and the house— even like this, it's such a friendly house," she said, filling her paper plate.

"We knew our friends wouldn't mind paper plates and paper cups, though Lexy thought plastic knives and forks was going too far." Sukie smiled. "Poor Lexy. We overruled her."

"Quite right, too. If you're all leaving today, who'd pack all that stuff?"

"Well, I bet Bertha wouldn't have minded. But she's done so much for us already, we decided not to ask." Sukie gestured at the neatly stacked cartons in one corner of the room, and Emma, standing in the doorway, smiled to see how black her fingernails were from weeding the garden. "Tomorrow she'll oversee the movers when they come to take all that to the barn, and all the furniture, too."

"You're lucky to have a good dry barn."

"Yes," said Sukie. "We've been very, very lucky about the farm, thanks to Jim Fothergill. Ma cared so much that we keep it in the family and Jim managed to do it. I wish he could have been here today."

Out on the lawn Pip said, "Come on, Cousin Horace, one last game of croquet."

Cousin Horace held out his hand. "Just get me to my feet, young feller," he said. "And I'll thrash you once again."

A little crowd gathered to watch the match. For a while the two players maintained a grim silence.

Each got his ball through the opening double wickets in one stroke, each hit flawlessly to and through the first single one. It was at the middle wicket that they clashed.

"Ah *Ha! Gotcha!*" yelled Pip as his ball nicked Cousin Horace's from twenty feet away.

He set the two balls side by side and, placing one foot heavily on his own, raised his mallet high, theatrically high, into the air.

"Now, let's see," he mused aloud. "Whither shall I banish thee? To the garden? The meadow? Whither, whither, whither? Ah, but of course! To the barn." And with a mighty blow he brought the mallet down.

"*Ow!*" yelled Pip, grabbing his foot and hopping wildly over the lawn. "*Ow! Ow! Ow!*"

Cousin Horace danced a little jig.

"Heh, heh, heh," he cackled. Standing over his ball, which had rolled only a few feet off course, he hit it smartly through the wicket. "Heh, heh, heh."

Emma was sitting under the tree-house maple, talking to Sonia Lunt, when Joey came and joined them. In a few minutes Sonia excused herself.

"It's getting on for milking time. I'd better collect Johnny," she said. "Again, happy birthday, Emma—no, don't get up—I don't like good-byes. You better come back next summer, come visit us." She smiled, though there were tears in her pretty green eyes. "It's been a lovely party, Emma, I believe the nicest one I ever went to. It's just like she's right here with us, having a good time, too. . . . Oh, there he is—Johnny! Come on, honey, it's milking time."

"Emma—" said Joey.

Emma put her hand on his arm. "Joey," she said. "Dear Joey. Have a wonderful senior year."

Lettie and Emma stood on the edge of the lawn, gazing down at the barnyard.

"I could hardly believe my ears when Jim told me," Emma said. "And I never really thanked you the day you came to get them."

"Well, Emma, if you all hadn't been so busy lately I'd have come over myself to suggest it, when I heard you were trying to place the horses."

"Thank heavens Jim called you."

"I'll say. . . . It's a shame he's not here today. Didn't your grandmother think the world of him?"

"Yes, she did; and it is a shame." A huge shame, thought Emma, wishing Jim were here to share with her this last good-bye. They had been through so much together at Bell Brook Farm.

"Listen, Em, did he tell you about the riding school?"

"Yes, Lettie, and I think it's wonderful."

"I'm going to start real slow, just my big feller— now that he's calmed down some—and Chloe, this fall. Then, if it works out, I'll add two more horses in the spring, and take in boarders. Maybe even by next June I'll need help, so you'd better keep me in mind for a summer job. You'd be my first choice, when I do hire someone."

"Thanks. Thanks a lot, Lettie. Next June seems so far off I can't believe it will ever happen."

"Sure, Em, that's natural. You've been through an awful lot this summer."

"Yes, well . . . it's just that right now I feel kind of muffled . . . or hobbled. It's not a bad feeling, but I can't seem to imagine any future. Maybe it has to do with leaving Bell Brook Farm. I hate that."

"God, Em, it must be hard . . . you're a good egg, d'you know that?"

Emma felt a lump in her throat. Around it she said, "*You're* a good egg, Lettie."

"Write me," said Lettie. "Write me after you get back to West Virginia and things kind of settle down. They will, Em."

"I guess so."

At the kitchen table sat Bertha and Joey's mother, Melissa Perry, barefoot, each with a glass of iced tea in her hand.

"I've always loved this kitchen." Melissa sighed. "The times I've sat here, talking to Gee, working things out when they'd get snarled at home . . . all day I've found myself looking for her, almost expecting to see her."

"Me, too," said Bertha.

Melissa drank some iced tea. "God knows we'll miss them all, the whole shooting match."

Just then Libba's George pounded through the room with Emma in hot pursuit. Giggling maniacally, he disappeared down the steps into the Music Room, and Emma flung herself onto Gee's old chair.

"Let Libba catch him if she can," she said. "Hello, Mrs. Perry."

"Hello, honey. How pretty you look. Was that necklace one of your birthday presents?"

Emma skewed her face down to admire the multicolored beads. "Yes," she said. "Pam gave them to me."

"Melissa and I were just saying how much we are going to miss you all," said Bertha, giving Emma's hand a little squeeze. "You know, when you girls told me you were going to have the party anyway, I thought, it'll never work. It's a big mistake. I was wrong, wrong as could be. It's a fine way to end things." Bertha patted Emma's hand. "And a fine way to send you home to West Virginia, birthday girl."

They looked at each other, until their eyes filled with tears.

"Oh, Bertha," said Emma.

Emma sat alone on the stone wall at the far end of the garden. For a while she watched the activity in the meadow, snorting inwardly when three of the aunts' husbands were struck out, one right after the other, by the sizzling pitches of Ray Flanagan. She noticed how long the shadows across the lawn had become and glanced at her watch.

After five, already. People were beginning to go. Near the Music Room door Mrs. Archer stood leaning on her cane, waiting for her daughter to bring up the car and searching the faces on the lawn.

She is looking for me, thought Emma. I should go say good-bye to her, but she did not move.

In the field the baseball game broke up.

Dr. and Mrs. Langdon and their daughter Polly were bidding the family good-bye on the lawn. When the last farewell was said, the last kiss exchanged, the Langdons started for the orchard pasture where their car was parked, and Emma saw that Joey was with them, walking with Polly. Emma smiled, but she felt a pang nonetheless.

"Good-bye," people called to each other on the shadow-barred lawn. "Good-bye, good-bye."

I'd better go up and get my stuff, Emma said to herself, but still she lingered a little longer, watching as the light from the descending sun, caught by the wall, filled the garden.

Sukie's left it looking nice, she thought. And out of the blue a memory tantalized her, a memory about the garden. Was it a dream? Sounds—the shouts of children, late birdsong—faded into the gentle glow around her. Emma looked down at the two old lawn chairs where Gee and Cousin Horace had sat the night they watched the July moon rise.

"I'm sure, pumpkin, that I can promise. I will be there for your birthday," she heard Gee say again, looking straight into Emma's eyes.

Emma felt the familiar sting across the bridge of her nose as tears blurred the garden and the familiar stab in her heart. She got up and started for the house, and one by one her mother and the aunts followed her inside and up the stairs to her room. Behind them, a moment later, came Pip and Dan.

Libba and Sukie were sitting on either end of Emma's trunk, trying to close it, when Matthew burst into the room.

"Look, Emma!" he crowed. "Look what's come for you! Another present! *Special Delivery* it says and they *did*. Mr. English drove it all the way out from Winslow—can you believe it?—on *Labor Day*!"

He held out a square package, with stickers saying *Fragile* in bold red and white on all four sides. Emma took it from him and looked it over.

"It's from New York," she said and read aloud the name of the store.

"Who from?" asked Pam from her perch.

"It doesn't say." Puzzled, Emma unwrapped the brown paper until it revealed a sturdy blue box. She set it down on top of her chest of drawers and raised the lid.

Inside the box was a nest of white tissue paper, in the middle of which Emma could feel her present. She lifted out the nest and held it a moment in both hands, trying to guess what it contained. Then she spied the little envelope lying on the bottom of the box; across it was written in a familiar hand, *For Emma on her birthday.*

"Who?"

"Who's it from?" cried Nell and Matthew and the aunts, and they gathered around her, leaving Dan and Pip to struggle with the trunk.

"Who, Em?"

"Oh, *do* hurry and open it."

But first Emma set down her present and took out the card and read to herself:

> *I looked and looked for something special for you. When I saw this in a little store on Third Avenue, just before going to the airport, I knew I had found it. Only after the owner wrapped it did I find out it's a music box, but I didn't have time to undo the package and listen. I hope you will play it for me sometime, Emma. Jim.*

"It's from Jim Fothergill," she said.

Deftly, quickly now, Emma unwrapped the

layers and layers of tissue paper until there, shed of its last covering, stood a china pig.

It was made of Gee's pink-and-white porcelain. Holding it before her, Emma drew in her breath. Her skin began to prickle.

"Oh, Em, *look*—it's Ma's china!" cried Lexy, and they all crowded nearer to look.

He was a perfect pig-pink with white dapples, and he stood on his hind legs, with one rear hoof cocked to set forth on a journey and a carefree smile on his rosy face. A blue china duffel bag was thrown over one shoulder, and a blue china sailor's cap was perched upon his head. Beneath him was a white china base.

"He's adorable," breathed Emma, and she remembered how they had laughed over the rooster and his book, and to herself she said, some day I will tell my children the stories about the rooster and the cow and the soup tureen, and they will tell theirs. . . .

Very, very carefully she began to turn her pig round and round while everyone watched in silence. Then she let go. Slowly the pig began to turn on its own, and then the tune started tinkling from the box.

Emma gasped. Every hair on her arms stood on end and her face went numb. Mutely, she looked around her and saw the family freeze, as though caught by the click of a camera.

"It's Gee's song," whispered Matthew, his eyes enormous.

"I don't believe it," said Sukie in a small voice, her grimy hand, holding a comb, motionless above her golden head.

"I do, Emma." Pip rose from the trunk and came across the room. "I do believe it. She promised."

And Emma, remembering again the garden, remembering the night Gee died and her farewell caress, whispered, "Me, too. I do believe it."

In the little room the music box plunked on and on and Emma began to sing, very softly, but very clearly, too:

"Sailing, sailing home *again,*
To see the girls upon the village green."

And one by one the others joined in:

"Then across the foam again,
To see the other seas we haven't seen."

until the little pig twirled slowly, slowly to a stop.

When the others had left her, bearing with them all her bags and baggage, Emma stood by her eastern window and gazed down at the empty barnyard. An early turned leaf fell from the maple at the southwest corner; a cheerful orange, it fluttered across the old sheep paddock and came to rest in the shadow of the barn.

Good-bye, barn.

To her right she could just see a corner of Gee's garden—a piece of the stone wall with the first bed beyond; and suddenly Emma remembered what had tantalized her when she sat there this afternoon.

It *was* a dream, she murmured. Last night I dreamed I watched Gee dancing in the garden. . . . She looked so well and free.

Good-bye, garden.

Turning from the window she regarded her room: her bed; the paper shepherdess upon the wall above it—the billowing skirt still now in the still room; the bureau that had housed the mouse (will he find it, in the barn? Emma wondered); the little pine desk. And she remembered her journal and said out loud, "But of course, of course I shall present my project. And I did a good job, too. I paid attention."

"Emma!" Pip's voice rose from the lawn. "We're all ready!"

"Good-bye, room. Good-bye, Bell Brook Farm," she whispered and waited for her heart to hurt.

When it did not, when instead she felt quite calm and full of peace, Emma recognized at last the difference that she had sensed within herself: For all her pain, fierce though it had been, the awful heavy dread was gone. It had been lifted from her the night Gee died.

Why on earth did I not realize that before?

Looking at the pig, Emma smiled.

How Gee must love the pig, she mused, remembering how her grandmother's eyes had sparkled when she told Emma and Jim about buying the cow in Normandy.

Then Emma thought again about the night Gee died. Never had she told anyone about the look of wonder on Gee's face nor the joy in her voice when Gee said yes. Never had she told anyone about lying in her bed afterward and feeling Gee move through her room; the touch on her head, the whisper in her ear.

Who would have believed her? Who would understand?

"Gee was going somewhere, the night she died. She was free," Emma said softly, in the same clear voice in which she had sung the song. "And I—"

"*Emma!* Come *on!*"

The front door slammed behind Pip, shaking the house, and the little sailor pig made a single slow turn on his stand. Was he going *home* again, or setting forth for seas he'd never seen?

Emma laughed.

"And I am going somewhere, too. I am free."

Oh, who could she tell, who would understand the wonderful peculiar news, that this summer had been the most important, the most beautiful time of Emma's life?

Pip, of course, but he already knew. She would talk to Pip someday.

Who could she *tell?* Who would explore it with her? Who would listen, who would hear?

Emma's heart gave a little hop.

Jim. Jim would understand.

Oh, *hurry* home, Jim, I have something wonderful to tell you.

And Gee? Did Gee know? Did Gee know all along, that Jim would understand? Of course. Of course, Gee knows.

Good-bye, Gee. Good-bye for now.

Emma picked up her precious pig and settled him in his nest and tucked the box under her arm. She went to the door and opened it.

"I'm coming, I'm coming," she called, running down the stairs; and for reasons that she both did and did not understand, her heart was as light as air.